OUTLAW
STRONGHOLD

Other books by S. J. Stewart:

Beyond the Verde River
Blood Debt
Fire and Brimstone
Gambler's Instinct
Outlaw's Quarry
Shadow of the Gallows
Vengeance Canyon

OUTLAW STRONGHOLD

•

S. J. Stewart

AVALON BOOKS
NEW YORK

Published by Avalon Books,
an imprint of Thomas Bouregy & Co., Inc.
160 Madison Avenue, New York, NY 10016

Library of Congress Cataloging-in-Publication Data

Stewart, S. J.
   Outlaw stronghold / S. J. Stewart.
      p. cm.
   ISBN 978-0-8034-7711-7
   I. Title.
   PS3569.T473O87 2010
   813'.54—dc22
                              2010022417

PRINTED IN THE UNITED STATES OF AMERICA
ON ACID-FREE PAPER
BY HADDON CRAFTSMEN, BLOOMSBURG, PENNSYLVANIA

Dedicated to the memory of my father-in-law,
Luther Orlean Stewart,
a man who had deep love for the Southwest

Chapter One

It had been a long, tiresome ride, and Cal Thornton was glad to be done with the transaction, though, as a rule, business was a pleasure. Now, however, all he wanted was a good meal and a warm bed. It was a casual remark that caught his attention and made him instantly alert.

"What did you say?" he demanded of Dewberry Potts, fixing the portly Wayside merchant with a stare. Potts gave him a questioning look. "About Marlow, I mean."

"Well, it's like I told you, I just got back a few days ago from doing some horse trading with an old buzzard, name of Marlow. He's got a place out west of town. It's less'n a day's ride."

Cal couldn't believe his luck. "Was his given name Tate?"

The merchant looked thoughtful. "Afraid I don't recall," he confessed, "but hold on a minute and I'll go look it up."

Potts turned and walked over to his desk where a

1

jumble of papers covered the top. He rummaged through most of them before coming up with a stained, crumpled scrap.

"Yep. It says right here on this bill of sale, 'Tate Marlow.' Nicely writ signature too. Have a look."

Cal did just that. It was Tate's scrawl, true enough. After all these years of searching, he'd found his friend and mentor, at last. He couldn't hide his elation.

"You must be a real good friend of his," said Potts.

"You could say that. He was closer to being my father, though. He took over the job after my pa died. I joined the Army in '62, and that was the last I saw of him. After the war, I tried to find him, but no one seemed to know where he went. He just disappeared. Maybe he thought I got killed or died of one of them diseases."

"Strange," said Potts. "I wouldn't have figured the old geezer to have any folks. Appeared to me he was one of them hermit types. You probably know him better than I do, but in case you've forgot; don't go sneaking up on him. He ain't the trusting kind."

This caused Cal to remember something Tate had said to him long ago. "Fellows who trust overmuch are apt to end up six feet under the sod."

"I'll be sure and announce my arrival," he said.

The two shook hands and Cal walked out of Potts' office a good deal richer, having sold his team of Percherons, along with an almost-new wagon and its load of merchandise that ranged from corsets to milk buckets. But best of all, he'd learned the whereabouts of Tate.

All he had left was his gear, his weapons, a tightly packed money belt, and a magnificent roan gelding named Coronado. Since it was growing late, he headed for the livery stable.

"Two dollars a night for you and your horse," said the hostler, an older fellow who moved as if he suffered from rheumatism. Cal handed it over. The livery stable looked cleaner than the local hotel. What's more, it was probably safer. That night he scarcely slept. As he tossed and turned, he kept thinking about the old man who'd done so much for him. It was Tate who'd patiently taught him how to read and write, and had seen to it that he had books. Truth was, Tate had taught him many things and had even saved his life once when a couple of border ruffians who didn't cotton to Kansans had jumped him.

By the time dawn was breaking over in the direction of Missouri, he had the big roan saddled and was ready to ride. At twenty-six, and a little taller than average, Cal Thornton was lean and well muscled from physical work. While his face was still youthful, there were lines at the corners of his steel-gray eyes from squinting into the sun. Since war's end, he'd made a good living traveling from one place to another, buying cheap and selling for a profit. To his way of thinking, it beat trailing a herd of cattle to the rails, or working on a railroad construction crew. It sure as the dickens beat farming.

As he rode across the grassy Kansas plain, he noticed that spring had settled in to stay a while. Overhead a flock of geese honked its way northward. It was a good day to be alive. He imagined how surprised Tate would be when he rode up to his place out of nowhere. After the greeting, there would be a lot of catching up to do. They had years to make up for.

The town of Wayside was far behind him when he topped a rise and reined up to have a look around. From this vantage point, he could see across the prairie for miles. A brisk wind rippled the great expanse of grass that stretched to the horizon. Unbidden, memories of his foster father filled his mind.

He'd been sixteen when he first laid eyes on the old man. It was the day his father died. Amos Thornton's horse was spooked by a water moccasin while crossing a rain-swollen Ozarks creek. He was thrown. His neck broke when he slammed against creek rock. Cal had watched, horrified. He jumped in and dragged his father back to the riverbank, but it was no use. He was dead. Tate happened along while he was sitting there, head in hands, blubbering like a two-year-old.

"It's a sorry thing to have happened," Tate sympathized. "But, son, we've got to get him buried."

The two of them took turns digging his father's grave. Afterward, Tate read words over it while Cal stood beside him, confused and forlorn. He could remember the sympathy in the older man's eyes when he put his hand on Cal's shoulder.

"Boy, if you haven't got any folks or any place to go, you're welcome to ride along with me."

Since he had neither folks nor a place to go, and hadn't the faintest idea what else to do, he'd tagged along. They moved westward into Kansas and got work when they could. When the work ran out, they rode on to some place else. It was during those years that Cal learned how to read. He learned a lot of other things too. In the evenings, Tate would talk about the happenings in the country, and about how war was brewing.

That wasn't exactly news to Cal after his near-fatal run-in with the ruffians from across the border. Tate also waxed eloquent about how a thinking man with ambition could become whatever he wanted. For a time, Cal was a believer.

The days slipped away, one after another, until the pain of his father's death had receded and was only a memory. They were living and working near the Kansas border when the war officially started. He'd been thinking about what he'd do in that event and was determined to join the Union Army. When he broke the news to Tate, the old man wasn't the least surprised.

"That's what I figured you was planning on doing, son," he said. "This sorry thing has been coming on for a long time. Best you get in there and help put an end to it."

They'd parted the next day at Mound City. "You take care of yourself, boy," he'd said as he shook Cal's hand. "Look me up when this thing is over."

That was the last he'd seen of the man who'd become a second father to him. After the war, he'd gone back to Mound City and asked around for him, but Tate Marlow had simply disappeared.

"Come on, Coronado," he said, nudging the big horse forward. "We're not going to get anywhere standing here gawking."

He came down off the hill and skirted a buffalo wallow. Back at Wayside, Potts had assured him that Tate's place was less than a day's ride. If so, he figured he'd be able to see it soon.

Sod houses tended to blend into the landscape, so he was close before he spotted it. It didn't look like much. None of them did. At the side, there was a lean-to for sheltering horses. It was half in and half out of a mound of earth. Trouble was, with no sign of mules or horses, the place appeared to be deserted. Cal was worried. Maybe Tate had pulled up stakes. He slipped out of the saddle and tied Coronado's reins to a support post.

"Hello in the house!" he called. "Tate, are you in there?" His only reply was the rattle of a stovepipe in the wind.

He approached the door with gun in hand. Taking a deep breath, he kicked it open. Cautiously, he stepped inside and glanced around the room. Not only was it empty of life, the place had been ransacked. Bedding was pulled from the bunk and strewn willy-nilly. Some of it was spattered with blood. So was the wall. Over in one corner lay a couple of books that had been left behind. He knelt and picked one up. Tate's name was scrawled on the front page. It was his copy of *Pilgrim's Progress*. The other was *Emerson's Essays*. Cal felt a lump in his throat. He'd read both of those very books.

No weapons had been left, and there was no food in the house. The thieves had taken everything they considered valuable. But most ominous was the blood. He feared for Tate's life. He hurried outside to have a look around. It was on the far side of the hill, behind the soddy, that he found his friend at last. Outlaws had knifed him. Then they'd dragged his body out back. Buzzards had kept away because the killers had wrapped him in a ground cloth. From the condition of the remains, he guessed the attack had occurred that morning, probably not long after he'd left Wayside. A wave of rage shot through him. It wasn't fair. After all these years, he'd been so close to a reunion, only to have it cruelly snatched away.

"Don't worry, my friend," he said. "I promise that if it's the last thing I do, I'll hunt your killers down. I'll make them pay for what they've done to you."

He buried Tate then. When it was done, he recited a few scriptures from memory. Then he walked away, leaving the last of his family in the bosom of the Kansas prairie.

Tracks near the stable indicated there'd been five of them. They'd approached from the northeast, not due east from Wayside. According to Potts, Tate had kept a mule and three fine horses. His weapons and everything else he owned were gone.

Cal took a measure of coffee and a soot-blackened pot from his belongings and went inside to build a fire. By the time this was done, the sun was sinking in the west. After a skimpy meal, he went out to care for Coronado.

"We're going to ride at first light, fella," he said. "Enjoy your rest."

Back inside, he threw his blankets on the bunk, crawled beneath them, and fell into a troubled sleep. He was awake before daylight. After fortifying himself with fried bacon and the last of the corndodgers, he packed his belongings, including Tate's books. The blanket roll, he tied behind the cantle. The books, he gently placed in one of the saddlebags. It was plain the outlaws were headed west. So was he.

He didn't think that Tate's place was the outlaws' destination. His old friend had been nothing more than a happenstance opportunity. It would take good luck and hard riding, but he was determined to catch up with them.

It was on the second day that he ran into trouble. He spotted a soddy in the distance, a place where he might pick up some information. When he approached, he was startled by the sound of a gunshot. Instinctively he slid from the saddle as if it had turned into a hot stovetop.

"Hey! Quit your shooting!" he yelled.

"Get on outta here, you dirty killer!" The voice came from a man who was belly-down on the soddy's roof.

Drawing his revolver, Cal hunkered low to make himself less of a target. He didn't think the shooter was likely to be one of the outlaws. They didn't know they were being followed and had no reason to leave a man behind to pick him off. Maybe he could talk his way out of this.

"You up there," he called. "I'm no killer. I'm just a stranger passing by."

The answer he got was a bullet. It landed close, plowing a furrow in the dirt. This was more than enough for Coronado. The big gelding took off like he'd been bit by a rattler, leaving his rider stranded.

Cal was close enough to use the .44. The angle wasn't good but he took a chance and squeezed off a shot. There was a yelp from the roof, meaning he'd struck flesh. A gun slid off and landed on the hard-packed earth below, followed quickly by the gunman. Cal waited for a time to see if he got up. He didn't.

He approached the downed sniper, cautiously, gun at the ready. The pistol that had tumbled was broken, probably beyond repair. The fellow who'd used it was out cold. With the toe of his boot, Cal turned him over. He looked like a kid. He was maybe fifteen, not more than sixteen. He was tall, almost as tall as Cal, but he was on the skinny side. It was as if his bones decided to grow all of a sudden and his flesh hadn't had a chance to catch up. He had a head of red hair and a face covered in freckles. There was a smear of blood at the hairline where the bullet had creased his scalp. Cal holstered his revolver and grabbed the kid under his arms. None too gently he dragged him into the house. There were two bunks stacked on one side. Cal hefted the boy onto the lower one. This elicited a moan. Whoever the redhead was, he appeared to be coming around. Cal found a rag that looked fairly clean. He dampened it with water from a half-full bucket that sat on a bench. He bathed the kid's face and washed the wound. It didn't look to be serious. When he was done, he searched the place for some alcohol or whiskey to ward off putrefaction. There was none to be found. The place had been picked clean, just like Tate's.

The kid moaned again and his eyelids fluttered open.

"What happened?" he mumbled.

"You shot at me. You shot twice, in fact. I returned the favor."

A look of alarm flashed across his freckled face. "Am I going to die?"

He sounded so melodramatic that Cal almost laughed. "Naw," he said. "You just got a scratch. Then you fell off the roof. I expect you're going to have a whale of a headache for a while, though."

The kid's look of fear instantly turned to one of hate. "Why did you kill my pa while I was away? There wasn't no call for that."

His hand groped for a pistol that wasn't there.

"I didn't kill your pa," said Cal. "I no more'n got here when you started slinging lead at me. The killers are long gone. I reckon I've got a good idea who they were, though."

The boy looked almost convinced. "Well, I'd sure like to know, if you'd be good enough to tell me."

"It was five outlaws. The same five that killed a good friend of mine the day before yesterday. After they knifed him, they stole his guns, horses, a mule, and whatever money he had."

"Did you see 'em?" he demanded to know, rising up on one elbow. "Can you put names to 'em?"

Cal shook his head. "Sorry, no. I wish I could, but I got there too late. I've been trailing them for nigh onto two days, though, and I figure they've got most of a day's lead on me."

"I should have been here," said the kid. "Pa sent me up to Morgan's to trade for a couple of mules, a horse, and some supplies. All the other times he's gone there himself and left me here to watch the place, but this time he sent me instead. He claimed I needed the experience."

Cal figured it had been a good thing for the boy. If he'd stayed at the soddy, he'd be dead. Still, he didn't expect that reminder would be a whole lot of comfort to a kid who'd just lost his father.

"My name's Cal Thornton," he said by way of introduction. "If I can help you, I'd be glad to."

It turned out the boy was Ross Hendrick, son of Mason Hendrick. His mother had died shortly after the family left Ohio for Kansas. Young Ross was alone now, and Cal was troubled by this. He didn't like riding off and leaving the kid to fend for himself. As it happened, Hendrick was thinking along those same lines.

"Take me with you," he pleaded as he swung his legs over the side of the bunk. "I want a chance at those killers."

Cal groaned inwardly. He didn't have the time or patience to nursemaid a green-behind-the-ears kid. Hendrick read his expression.

"See here, Mr. Thornton, I can help you track them down. And if you'll think about it, two against five is better odds than one against five."

Depends on who the two men are, Cal thought.

"Look, Hendrick," he said with all the patience he could muster, "these outlaws are dangerous. You've seen what they can do."

"I've seen. I buried my pa a little while ago. But there's nothing I want more in this world than to make those killers pay for what they've done."

Cal understood his need for justice. He felt the same way. Hendrick reminded Cal of himself when he was a scared and lonely kid. It was Tate who'd been there for him. There was no way he could pay his debt to that kindly old man, but maybe he could do for Hendrick what Tate had done for him.

"Look," he said, "if you're sure this is what you want, I guess you can tag along."

He watched the kid's expression brighten.

"However," he said sternly, "you're going to have to

do what I tell you. I won't stand for you losing your temper, or ignoring my orders and doing something stupid that could get us both killed."

"I understand," the boy said.

"Good. Then I need to borrow one of your horses so I can go after mine. Coronado bolted when you got trigger happy."

"Sure. Help yourself."

"While I'm rounding up my horse, get packed and ready to go. We're hitting the trail as soon as I get back."

Cal went out to the stable and saddled a long-legged gray. Then he headed north, following Coronado's tracks. It didn't take him long. The horse was already on its way back now that the ruckus had stopped.

Back at the soddy, he fished a half-spent bottle of whiskey from one of his saddlebags. Then he called to Hendrick. The kid had just finished packing the supplies he'd bought at Morgan's on the mules.

"Hold still while I pour some whiskey on that wound," Cal said.

When the alcohol hit the raw place, Hendrick cringed, but he was game. After bandaging the kid's head, they were ready to ride.

On the far side of the stable, he noticed a fresh mound of earth. A crude wooden cross marked the head of the grave. No doubt it was the final resting place of the elder Hendrick.

Between them, he and Ross Hendrick had three horses and two mules. Thanks to the kid's supplies, they were well fixed. He had no side arm, but he did have a new-looking Winchester. Along with Cal's Smith & Wesson .44 and Winchester rifle, they were fairly well armed.

"What were you and your father planning to do here?" said Cal once they were on their way. "Farm?"

"Actually, we were going to build us a herd."

"Funny. I didn't see nary a cow."

"We hadn't got 'em yet. Pa was going to ride out, find a herd, and buy their newborns. They say you can get them cheap because they're a hindrance."

"What were you going to do until they grew up and built a herd?" he asked, thinking that the boy's father hadn't thought things through very well.

"Pa had set a little money aside. We could afford to wait. At least we could until those no-accounts robbed and killed him."

Cal figured the Easterner had known as much about cattle ranching as Cal knew about sewing women's dresses. He guessed the old saying was true, that fools rush in where angels fear to tread.

"How are we going to catch up to the killers if they're always so far ahead?" said Hendrick.

It was a good question, and thanks to the kid, he'd fallen even farther behind than before.

"They're bound to stop somewhere," he said. "When they do we'll make up the difference."

His new partner didn't appear especially reassured by this.

Cal waited until it was fully dark before he stopped. By the light of the moon, they made a cold camp on the lee side of a rise. He expected Hendrick to complain. He didn't. The boy chewed on some jerked beef and dried apples. Then he crawled into his blankets. Before dawn, they'd packed up and were on their way again.

On the second night, Cal built a small fire in a bowl-shaped depression. There, the two of them were enjoying a hot meal when Cal heard a faint noise. His hand closed on the grips of his pistol just as a voice called out, "Hello the camp."

He scrambled to his feet, wary of any stranger. "Come on in if you're friendly," he said.

A lone man walked into the circle of firelight. He was stocky, with long, shaggy hair and a beard to match. He carried a shotgun with the barrel resting across one arm. A glance told Cal that this fellow wasn't a pilgrim.

"Smelled your coffee," he said. "Sure was a temptation."

"Help yourself to what's left," said Cal. "There's some bacon in the skillet if you're hungry."

"Don't mind if I do."

The stranger filled his coffee cup and took the rest of the bacon and fry bread.

"Did you come from the west?" asked Cal.

"Yep."

"You didn't happen to see a gang of five men, did you?"

"Matter of fact, I saw 'em earlier today. They were a good distance away and angling southward. I'm glad they weren't heading in my direction. I've got me half a dozen broke horses that I'm taking up to Fort Dodge. Might have been a temptation to an outfit of that size."

Cal didn't doubt it.

"Where are the horses now?" asked Hendrick, looking around and sniffing the air.

"Left 'em back a ways. Staked 'em so they wouldn't

take off whilst I was gone. And dag-burn it, that coffee's hot! 'Course that's the way I like it."

An idea occurred to Cal about how he could get the other mount he needed.

"Could you be persuaded to sell me one of those horses?" he asked.

The stranger scratched his whiskers. "Well, maybe. If you can pay the price."

They couldn't do any horse-trading in the dark, so Cal invited him to share their campfire for the night.

"Nope," he said. "I like my own company and I want to keep an eye on my horses. But I'll be back come daylight and I'll bring 'em with me."

True to his word, the man showed up just as the sun was starting to rise. Cal dickered for a handsome zebra dun that he picked out from the rest. They came to an agreement on price. He pocketed the bill of sale that had been scribbled hastily on a sheet from a tally book and signed "Fitzsimmons."

"You wouldn't be figuring on the two of you taking on them five riders by yourselves?" Fitzsimmons asked.

"They're killers as well as thieves," said Cal. "They killed my best friend and this boy's pa. We'll trail them to wherever they're going. After that, we'll see."

"Then I wish you good hunting."

"And you a safe trip to Fort Dodge," said Cal.

He and Hendrick mounted up. They rode off in one direction, Fitzsimmons in the other. It wasn't long before they found the place where the outlaws' tracks angled southward.

"Hey, Thornton, do you think they're headed for no-man's-land?" said Hendrick.

"It looks that way."

"Pa said that was a bad place."

Cal agreed. The strip of land that separated Kansas from Texas was lawless. Only a federal marshal or a deputy federal marshal had jurisdiction, and both were scarce as hen's teeth. The place drew outlaws like molasses drew ants.

"Let's hope those five aren't heading for Outlaws' Roost," he said. "Once there, we'd never stand a chance of getting to them."

Hendrick looked stricken. "Do you think that's where they're going?"

"Something tells me they're not," he said thoughtfully. "The way they're traveling, I think they're going somewhere for a purpose. If it was their intention simply to hide out and take it easy, they wouldn't be in such a hurry."

"I sure hope you're right, Thornton."

He wasn't the only one. Outlaws' Roost was an impregnable fortress.

Cal was ambivalent about his decision to bring Hendrick along. It might be that he'd made a mistake. Still, the only other choice was to have left him on his own, and bullheaded as Hendrick was, he'd probably have followed anyway.

For a time the kid was quiet, seeming to be lost in thought. He broke the silence with a question. "Are you scared, Thornton?"

Cal glanced at him. "Guess I'd be a fool not to be," he replied. "But whatever happens, tracking down those killers is something I have to do."

"Yeah, I know. I feel the same way. I don't see how

my pa can rest easy until those no-accounts pay for what they've done."

"Then I expect we'd better not lose their trail."

They were making better time now that he could switch from Coronado to the zebra dun. It was a fine horse, maybe not as good as Coronado was, but it had a lot of staying power.

It was well into the afternoon when the sun disappeared behind a bank of low clouds. Rain began to fall, lightly at first. Then it came down in sheets. Thunder rumbled across the high plains and an occasional lightning bolt shot from the darkened sky. Cal shrugged deeper into his waterproof poncho. Hendrick had donned his slicker. He wished for shelter as the cold rain pelted his face. There was none to be had. The only thing to do was ride out the storm. Eventually the rain tapered off.

"Looks like their tracks are all washed out," said Hendrick, clearly dismayed. "What are we going to do now?"

"I think I know where they're headed," said Cal. "Don't worry. We'll pick up their trail again."

"Where are they going?"

"Not to Texas, that's plain enough. The way I figure it, they're headed due west toward New Mexico Territory."

Hendrick looked skeptical. "Again, I hope you're right, Thornton."

"So do I, amigo. So do I."

Chapter Two

Cal sat on his haunches, warming his hands by the campfire. It had been years since he'd left Tate back in Mound City to go off to war. And yet the old man's death had hit him hard. The brutal way he'd died only hours before their intended reunion was a torment.

"Isn't that coffee and bacon ready yet?" said Hendrick. "I'm hungry enough to eat an armadillo, hide and all."

Cal wondered how a boy with his appetite could stay so rail thin and concluded it was one of nature's mysteries.

"Keep your britches on," he said. "It won't be long, now."

When they'd finished eating, they threw down their ground covers and rolled out their blankets. The storm had long since moved on to the east, leaving behind a clear, star-filled sky.

Cal was beginning to drift off to sleep when he heard

muffled sobs coming from beneath Hendrick's covers. He felt a rush of sympathy. For sure, the kid had plenty of reason to grieve, having lost his pa and left his home all on the same day. Not to mention that he'd also been wounded, even if the injury had been minor. Circumstances were forcing Ross Hendrick to grow up fast.

Cal thought again of his own loss. When he'd learned of Tate's whereabouts from Potts back in Wayside, he'd felt like a kid on Christmas morning. It was a blow to find his Christmas stocking empty. How badly he'd wanted to see Tate again, to feel, once more, that he had a family. But wallowing in sadness wasn't helping matters a bit. He deliberately shut down his thoughts and slipped into a deep sleep.

They broke camp at first light. The rain of the previous day had settled the dust. Everything around them smelled fresh and clean.

"You can see forever out here," said Hendrick, when they were under way. "You'd think we'd be able to spot those five riders when they've only got a day's lead."

"The land can fool you. It isn't as flat as it looks. There's dips and gullies you'd never suspect. Besides, they've probably gotten further ahead of us."

"I sure hope you're wrong, Thornton. About them widening the gap, I mean."

They rode in silence for a time before Hendrick came up with another question.

"What's to keep us from losing them altogether? Since the storm wiped out their tracks, we don't even have a trail to follow."

"We know they're heading west," he explained. "So we're going to keep riding in the same direction."

"Guess we've got no choice."

It was on the second morning after the storm that they caught sight of a bedraggled cluster of tents.

"What do you suppose that is?" said Hendrick, standing in his stirrups to get a better look.

"It appears that some folks have made a camp."

The collection was a ragtag affair consisting of several patched tents and a few animals. A tattered Stars and Bars was tacked to a makeshift flagpole. Out front two young boys played with a yapping little dog.

"You don't suppose those killers are in there?" said Hendrick.

Cal glanced over at the boy and noted his tenseness. He would have bet money that he was steeling himself to ride into that camp, gun drawn.

"Settle down, Hendrick. They're not there."

"How do you know that?"

"First off, their horses aren't around. Second, they wouldn't have stayed this long even if they'd stopped for grub. They've got someplace they need to get to."

Hendrick reined up and called after him.

"At least we're going over and asking a few questions, aren't we? Whoever's there might be able to tell us something."

The place was too quiet and seemingly empty of men. They were either hiding in ambush, or the women and children were alone and would be unnerved by their intrusion.

"We're going to cut a wide berth," he said. "I don't

expect those outlaws rode up and introduced themselves polite-like, anyway. So we're not going in there frightening a bunch of women and kids."

When Hendrick caught up, he was mumbling under his breath. Cal caught the word "dumb" and a few other words that Mrs. Hendrick, rest her soul, would've been shocked to hear on the lips of her son. Still, he kept his promise to do what he was told without argument.

Keeping their distance from the tent settlement, they rode on by. The dog noticed them and started barking. This alerted another mutt who joined in. The ruckus caused a woman in blue calico to lift a tent flap and come out. Several others joined her. The women stared in their direction, shielding their eyes with their hands. The boys stopped playing for a moment and watched the strangers ride by. After one called out to them, the woman hustled them inside. Beyond the encampment, Cal picked up the trail again, one that had been made after the storm. Only this time there were more than five sets of tracks. A lot more.

"What does this mean?" Hendrick wondered aloud. "Did they get men from the camp to join them?"

"I'm not sure what's going on," he confessed, "but I expect we'll find out."

He didn't like to think that the five outlaws had more than tripled in number. If this was the case, it was going to make his job a lot harder, perhaps impossible. A couple of hours had passed when Cal spotted a band of riders heading toward them.

"Uh-oh, get ready for trouble," said Cal, pulling back on the reins of the zebra dun. Hendrick drew up beside him. It was plain the kid was scared. His face was ghost-pale in every place there wasn't a freckle. Truth be known, he was uneasy himself.

"Thornton, I don't like this," Hendrick said, his voice a high-pitched squeak.

"Don't like it much, myself. Get ready. But don't do anything unless I tell you."

Together they watched the riders approach. Cal counted a dozen men of different ages and sizes. He could see that the horses had been ridden hard. When they drew near, they fanned out. Hendrick's rifle lay casually across his lap. His own hand was near the grips of his .44.

"What's your business?" demanded a gaunt, shabbily clad elder who wore a Confederate campaign hat.

"We're on the trail of five killers," said Cal. "I don't suppose you've seen them?"

"Might have," he said. "What do they look like?"

Cal admitted he didn't know. "We were following their trail."

"Well, we've seen 'em. They stopped and made trouble for our people. You must have noticed our tents back yonder."

Cal nodded. "We rode on by without stopping. Didn't figure there was any sense in worrying the women and children."

"I appreciate that," said the elder, whose expression softened a bit. "The outlaws were going to rob us of our horses. More than that, I didn't like the way that young one was leering at my daughter. They acted as if they owned the place 'til they noticed there was some of us hid out in a gully with guns and a willingness to use 'em. Let's say we persuaded them to leave. Then we saddled up and followed to make sure they kept on going."

In spite of their poverty, the Southerners could take care of their own. He respected that.

"I'd guess they're about a day ahead of us," he said.

"That's about right."

"I'd be obliged if you could give me their descriptions."

"Be glad to. Two were big hombres, but one was even bigger than the other was. He had fists like hams that could kill a man easy. Another was a little runt with squinty eyes. One was young and mean. He was the one eyeing my girl. The fifth was ordinary. Nothing about him was different enough to make you remember. All of 'em wore beards. They had a bunch of real fine horses with 'em. Wouldn't surprise me to hear they were stolen."

"They were," said Cal, thinking of Tate's missing livestock. "At least some of them were."

"Are you fellows the law?"

"Here in the strip?" said Cal. "No. This is a personal matter. They killed someone very close to us."

"Then I wish you Godspeed," he said. "They're vermin on the land."

"We're obliged for the information," said Cal, touching the brim of his hat in salute. He rode through the opening they made for him then. Hendrick followed close behind. Neither of them looked back until he heard their horses ride off in the distance.

He'd made progress. They had the killers' descriptions.

While Cal had never been to the West, at least not

farther than eastern Kansas, he'd listened to others who had. Mostly they were teamsters on the Santa Fe trade route. But there'd been others too. While he didn't exactly have a detailed map in his head, he wasn't riding blind, either.

He spotted the landmark in the distance the following day. "Rabbit Ears" was the name the teamsters and other westward-movers had given it. He pointed it out to his partner.

"Know what that means?"

"Uh, no."

"That's New Mexico Territory up ahead."

"So they were headed for New Mexico all the time."

Landmarks are visible from great distances in open country, so it was two days before they even drew close to the two upthrusts of rock.

After they'd passed the Rabbit Ears, the land became arid. Cal noticed that the air he breathed felt lighter, somehow. On the western horizon, a mountain range loomed. It stretched as far north and as far south as the eye could see. They rode through a landscape thickly dotted with yucca spikes and clumps of chamisa. Cal's teamster friends had talked of these things. They told how the Indians made soap from the yuccas, and that they had other uses for them, as well. They described how chamisa would yellow up in the fall and carpet the land in gold. He figured that would be a sight worth looking at.

With every mile past Rabbit Ears, Hendrick's impatience grew. He complained because of the miles they'd ridden. He complained because they were no closer to a showdown. In general, he complained.

"Look here, Thornton," he said, "are they ever going to stop so we can catch up? Or are we kidding ourselves?"

Instead of answering right off, Cal pulled back on the reins and dismounted. Then he took his time checking Coronado's front shoe. It gave him a chance to get hold of his temper and choose the words he wanted to use.

"I told you this wasn't going to be a church social. You must have known you were in for saddle sores and aggravation. As for the outlaws, wherever they go, we'll be on their trail. When they do decide to stop, we'll catch them."

The kid looked unconvinced.

"If you don't like it, you can always turn around and head back to Kansas," he said. "I can do this alone."

Hendrick looked like he'd been slapped. "I'm sticking," he said. "It's just that it's taking so long."

"It's apt to be a gunfight when we catch up. If we can't get the law to help, I'm not going to let them get away with what they did."

Again, he felt guilty about bringing the orphaned boy along on a manhunt that might well end in his death.

Hendrick settled down after letting off steam. There was no more trouble before they reached the dusty town of Las Vegas that lay sprawled near the southern end of the mountains. Since this might well be the outlaws' final destination, Cal was alert.

"What do we do now?" said Hendrick, gawking at everything as if he'd never seen a town before. "I sure wish those men could have given us the killers' names. It would make finding them a lot easier."

"No doubt. But like Tate used to say, 'If wishes were horses, beggars would ride tall in the saddle.'"

What he did know was that five killers had ridden into Las Vegas. If they were still in town, he intended to find them. One of the horses he'd been trailing had a distinctive right front shoe, something he'd noticed at Tate's soddy. In addition to the descriptions he already had, it should be enough.

"We'll take a turn around the plaza," he said. "Maybe we can spot them."

So many businesses surrounded the street that circled the parklike square that there was no way to pick out an individual track from among the many. Neither was there five men fitting the descriptions the Southerners' had given.

A teamster once told him that Kearney had stood on one of the flattop roofs when he informed the people that New Mexico had been taken by the United States. He wondered which building had served as Kearney's platform. They all looked very much alike.

"Find what you were looking for?" said Hendrick after they'd made the round.

"No."

"So, now what?"

"Now, we do a little shopping."

"What for?"

It was a dumb question as far as Cal was concerned.

"Look, the parts of your clothes you haven't worn through, you've grown out of. You're starting to look like a redheaded scarecrow that's escaped from somebody's cornfield."

Hendrick flushed in embarrassment. "I've got no money and I sure ain't got credit."

"We're partners. Don't worry about money."

They hitched the horses and mules in front of the general merchandise store and went inside. The place was well stocked and smelled like all general merchandise stores. Inside, the scents of leather, peppermint, and coffee mixed with a dozen others. Cal pulled two sets of clothes apiece from the shelves. Then he added a pair of boots for Hendrick, who'd taken to store buying like geese took to the sky. When he went to pay for his purchases, he had the storekeeper add a box of cartridges.

"Wish I still had my pistol," Hendrick muttered, eyeing one of the weapons the merchant had on display.

Cal ignored the hint.

Back on the street, the kid looked at him questioningly. "Where do we go now?"

"Let's head for the livery stable. The animals need tending, and after all those days cropping grass, they deserve a bait of oats."

"You given up on finding my pa's killers?"

"Nope," he said, as he mounted up. "If they stopped here, there's a good chance the hostler has seen them."

Hendrick's expression brightened. "That sounds reasonable," he agreed.

It didn't take them long to find the place they were looking for. It was on one of the side streets that led away from the plaza.

"What can I do for you gents?" said the hostler, wiping his hands on the sides of his pants as he came forward to greet them. He was an older fellow with a paunch and a drooping mustache.

"We need to grain-feed and rub down the animals," said Cal, "and we're looking for some information."

At the word "information," the man got a whole lot less friendly looking.

"I can take care of your animals," he said. "But around here a fellow could get killed for shooting off his mouth."

"We're leaving Las Vegas at first light," Cal assured him. "Nobody will ever know you said anything." He pulled out a two-dollar gold piece and displayed it on his open palm. The hostler was clearly tempted.

"All right," he said, "go ahead and ask your questions. If I feel I can answer, I will."

"Fair enough. My partner and I are after the five outlaws that killed his pa and a friend of mine. We trailed them here to Las Vegas. Two of 'em are big fellows. One is a runt with squinty eyes. One is young and looks real mean. The last fellow is ordinary. Oh, and one of the horses has a noticeable nick in its right front shoe."

The hostler stroked his mustache as if trying to make a decision. "I reckon I know the ones you're talking about," he said at last. "They're ahead of you by more'n a day. They pulled out yesterday. I have to admit I was glad to see the last of 'em."

"Can you give me their names?"

The man eyed the gold piece that Cal was still holding.

"A couple, I guess. The biggest man appeared to be the boss. His hands were huge. Deadly weapons, they were. One of his men called him Barley. The least one in size was called McGill."

"And the other three?" Cal prompted.

"Afraid I can't put names to 'em. You're right about the young one being mean. I could see it in his eyes. The way he talked you'd think he was always trying to start something. It was him that worried me more than any of the others."

"Thanks," said Cal, dropping the coin into the man's hand. He figured he'd earned it. "Did they say where they were going from here?"

"Not to me. But I overheard one of 'em talking to another, and he mentioned they were heading for Santa Fe. They were supposed to find somebody there."

"They say who it was?"

"Nope. They just said it was somebody they had to find. Now, I've got to get back to work."

"If you've got room enough, we'd like to stay here tonight," said Cal.

"You can sleep in the loft. It'll be a dollar apiece for the two of you and four dollars for the horses and mules."

Cal fished in his vest pocket and came up with the money. It went to join the two-dollar gold piece.

"There's a pump out back if you fellows want to clean up," he said, as he returned to work.

They went outside and managed to wash off most of the trail dust. Cal's stubble had grown into a respectable beard. He ran his fingers through it while considering a visit to a barber. In the end, he decided not to bother. As for the kid, his peach fuzz was scarcely worth the two bits it would cost to remove it.

After they'd cleaned up, Cal retrieved the packages he'd bought at the mercantile, and they climbed into the loft to change.

"Well, how do I look?" said Hendrick, once he was outfitted in new clothes.

Cal glanced at him. "I have to admit you look a whole

sight better now that your britches come all the way down to your feet."

"Yeah. And I really like the boots. Thanks."

"You can pay me back one of these days when you're a rich rancher, or whatever it is you take a notion to do."

"It's not likely I'll ever be rich. I ain't much good at anything. I wasn't even good at horse trading, but Pa had hopes."

"Looks like you did all right to me. Besides, a fellow gets better with practice at anything he does. Don't give up on yourself. I expect you'll do fine."

He blushed to the roots of his red hair. "Thanks for saying so."

As Cal finished dressing, he thought about how much Hendrick reminded him of himself in his younger years. He'd been just as unsure and every bit as self-conscious.

"Well, now that we're all spruced up," he said, "why don't we go get something to eat. I saw a café on the plaza. Close as it is, we can walk over."

It was a little too early for the evening trade, so except for three fellows at the other end of the room, they had the place to themselves.

"What'll you gents have?" asked the graybeard who was taking orders.

"Venison steak, biscuits, and gravy," Cal ordered. "And lots of coffee. Hot and black."

Hendrick ordered the same. He was always hungry. But then he was all bones and sinew, and had a lot of fleshing out to do.

They were making inroads on the gravy-covered steaks when Cal got an uneasy feeling that he was being watched. He glanced up to find that the men across the room were looking him and Hendrick over. Something was on their minds and it wasn't apt to be good.

The kid was hard to distract when he was busy with a fork, but he noticed too. He nudged Cal with his foot. "Those fellows keep staring at us," he said under his breath. "I wonder why?"

"Ignore them," Cal whispered. "They might be trying to start something."

He didn't want to meet their gazes and give them an excuse to cause trouble. Still, he managed to sneak an occasional glance every once in a while. By the time the meal was over, he could give good descriptions of each of them.

After wiping his mouth, he called the graybeard over to pay him.

"That was a fine meal," he said. "Best I've had in New Mexico."

"I'm glad you enjoyed it, sir, and I'll tell the cook."

One of the three at the other end of the room sniggered. Cal pretended he didn't hear. The waiter, sensing trouble, scurried off to the kitchen. Cal was prepared for trouble when he scooted his chair back and got up. But without so much as a glance in their direction, he left the restaurant. Hendrick was right behind him.

"What do you think about those fellows in there, Thornton?" he said when they were out of earshot.

"They're up to no good. I wouldn't be surprised if they followed us to see where we're staying."

"You think they're planning to rob us?"

"Look at it this way. We're strangers in town. We've got new clothes and spending money. They've got to figure we have at least two horses and the gear to go with them. They've gone and sized us up as easy pickings."

"Job's boils, we don't need this," Hendrick swore, kicking up street dirt with the toe of his new boot.

Cal agreed. Still, what you didn't need, you sometimes got anyway.

When they were about to turn off the plaza onto a side street, he paused and bent as if to pick up a coin from the dirt. When he straightened, he half turned and opened his hand as if showing Hendrick his find. When he did so, he could see they were being observed by the trio, who were standing in front of the café.

"Are they there?" said Hendrick, keeping his voice low.

"Yep. They're watching us. I expect we're going to have visitors come dark."

"Does this mean we're going to have to sit up all night?"

"Maybe not. Let's get back to the livery stable. I've got an idea."

As soon as it was dark enough to provide cover, he climbed down from the loft where he'd spread his blankets. Moonlight spilled from a high opening, allowing him to see his way.

"Where are you going?" said Hendrick. "Can I come along?"

"No. I need you to stay here and keep an eye on things. I won't be long."

He grabbed a burlap bag from a nail before slipping through the doorway. Outside he paused and glanced around. There was no sign of the would-be robbers. He made his way stealthily toward the plaza. He kept to the shadows until he reached the back of one of the saloons. Light poured from a crack at the bottom of the ill-fitting door, so it didn't take long for him to find and collect what he was looking for. He filled the burlap bag with empty whiskey bottles. Walking carefully, so as not to clink the glass bottles against one another, he retraced his steps.

When he entered the livery barn, he found Hendrick waiting impatiently at the foot of the ladder.

"Now, do you mind telling me what this is all about?" he said.

"A little backup is all. Watch and learn."

Cal took half the bottles and piled them at the front opening. If they were to have unwanted visitors during the night, they would announce themselves by tripping over the glass and making a lot of noise. He stacked the rest of the bottles at the backdoor. Then he gave the bag a shake and replaced it on its nail.

Hendrick was impressed. "Wish I'd thought of that trick," he said.

"Afraid I can't take the credit. It was taught to me by a fine old man."

"The one that was murdered?"

"Yeah. One and the same."

"So, what now?"

"Now, we climb up that ladder and get some shuteye. I expect it will be a while before our company gets here. They'll want to give us time to fall asleep so they can catch us unawares."

He had his pistol beside him when he bedded down. The knife he'd taken from his saddlebag was also near at hand.

"I haven't got a pistol," Hendrick reminded him. "What do you expect me to do, throw a whiskey bottle at 'em?"

"You've got your rifle. Use that if you need to. But don't start shooting 'til I say so."

He grumbled some about the country being full of killers and thieves, and about being without a respectable firearm. Then he fell asleep. Cal took longer to drift off.

He couldn't have slept more than a couple of hours before he heard the crash and tinkle of broken glass, followed by a stifled curse. He grasped the Smith & Wesson and crawled forward to where he could look down. The front door was open a crack and a cold wind blew into the barn. Just then the back door flew open and the other pyramid of glass came crashing down.

"What in blazes happened?" said one of the would-be thieves, unmindful that he could be heard by anyone in the barn.

"Shut up!" was his answer.

Cal saw the outline of the three of them bathed in moonlight. "Drop your guns!" he ordered.

They looked up, trying to locate the speaker.

"He's got us, Coble. Don't go getting us shot."

"Better listen to him," Cal warned. "I'm not telling you again to drop your guns and keep your hands in sight."

Reluctantly they obeyed.

"Now, get down there and collect their weapons, Hendrick, and stay out of the line of fire."

The boy scrambled down the ladder and collected the guns. When this was done, Cal joined him.

"There's some rawhide strips in one of my saddle-bags," he said. "Go get them and tie their hands."

Hendrick hesitated. "Shouldn't we roust out the local law? They could give us a hand with these coyotes."

The heftiest of the outlaws laughed. "You two are sure a couple of greenhorns," he said. "The local law is a friend of ours. Get him over here, and he'll haul your backsides to jail quicker than you can put your boot in a stirrup. Then we'll divide up whatever you've got, giving the town marshal his cut, of course."

So that's the way it is.

"Do you think he's telling the truth?" said Hendrick, who wasn't entirely convinced.

"Hey, ask old Loftis over there," said the outlaw. "He'll tell you."

Cal suspected they were a little too cocky to be running a bluff. Even if they were, there was no way he could take a chance that the local law wasn't crooked. If he was wrong, he could lose everything, including the killers.

"Take their bandanas and gag 'em," he ordered. "I'll check the bindings."

"You ain't gaggin' me . . . ," said the one called Loftis, as the deed was being done.

"Now, get the horses saddled and the mules packed," Cal ordered after the trio were secure. "I've got to gather up these whiskey bottles and glass shards."

"Why bother?"

"Because a piece of broken glass is heck on leather strips, and I want these fellows to stay put as long as possible."

"Guess I didn't think of that."

"Before you start, take one of their pistols for yourself. I'm sure you can put it to better use than its owner has. Besides, I figure they owe us a weapon for the trouble they've caused."

Hendrick picked one out and threw the others outside.

By the time Cal had the whiskey bottles and pieces of glass gathered up and sacked, Hendrick had Coronado saddled and was tightening the cinch on his own mount.

"Boys," he said to the hogtied outlaws, "you ought to take up a line of honest work. You're sure not any good at this one." He figured it was just as well they couldn't answer.

They rode out of Las Vegas in the dead of night. Cal cradled the sack of glass bottles so they wouldn't rattle, while Hendrick took charge of the lead ropes. About a mile out of town, Cal tossed the sack, looking back as he did. The only lights were those from the saloons.

"How much time do you think we've got?" said Hendrick.

"Maybe 'til dawn, when the hostler comes in to work."

"Then I guess we'd better get a move on."

Nobody had to urge Cal. He wanted to put as much distance between them and Las Vegas as he possibly could. There was trouble enough waiting for them up ahead.

Chapter Three

They loped their horses in the direction of Santa Fe by the light of the moon and a thousand low-hung stars. Cal didn't mind riding at night, especially when each minute brought him closer to Tate's killers. They'd had a close call and they'd been lucky. Still, he didn't think for a minute they'd seen the last of the Las Vegas outlaws.

Hendrick, having kept quiet as long as his nature would allow, spoke up. "I'm worried that this Barley fellow and his pals will find who they're looking for in Santa Fe and be long gone by the time we get there."

His fear was justified. Still, it was rumored there were temptations in the old town to detain such men who'd long been on the trail. Tequila, pretty girls, good food, and games of chance could all serve to hold a man for a time.

"I think I may know a shortcut through the mountains," said Cal, squinting ahead in the darkness.

"What? I thought you'd never been here before."

"I haven't. But I've talked to them that have. I knew

a fellow back in Kansas who drove a team of mules to Santa Fe. He told me about this short cut. Never took it himself, but learned of it from a man who had."

Old Ned Mayhew knew just about everything there was to know about getting a wagon load of freight between Westport and Santa Fe. He'd learned a lot about the Southwest and had quit because of his rheumatism. He was helping his brother run a general store in Mound City when Cal got to know him.

"Well, if you can spot a mountain trail in no more light than what we've got, your eyes are better than mine," said Hendrick.

"I expect it'll be daylight before we reach it." Cal's hope lay in finding that shortcut. Going through the mountains instead of riding around the southern end would save them precious time.

"Maybe that outfit from Las Vegas won't come after us once they get loose," said Hendrick.

"Oh, they'll come all right. We humiliated them and made them look like bungling fools. They're not going to let that pass."

"I guess not," he conceded. "They were probably telling the truth about the local law being crooked too."

"It doesn't matter. Either way, we couldn't risk it. There's too much at stake to take the chance of being robbed and jailed."

"I wish they'd picked on somebody else. We seem to be attracting trouble."

They rode side by side then without talking. Cal's face felt the bite of the cold spring wind that blew down from the snowcapped mountain. He was grateful for it. It kept him alert.

"Why do you reckon that some fellows go bad and kill people, good people who never did anything to hurt 'em?" said Hendrick as if he'd been pondering this for a while.

The question caught Cal off guard.

"I guess folks have been wondering about that ever since Cain murdered Abel. Afraid I don't have an answer. Leastwise, not one that makes much sense."

What he'd learned was there were men who placed a low value on human life other than their own. It was nothing short of arrogance. Then there was a kind of man who had something twisted inside his head. These were the sort who'd taken pleasure in killing during the war. When it ended, and they had no further mandate, they couldn't seem to stop. For them, robbing people, banks, or railroads—and killing bystanders—was simply a way to satisfy their bloodlust. To his way of thinking, they were loco.

They rode until there was a promise of sunrise. A glance at their back trail told him that no one was following. Not yet, anyway.

"Look sharp," he said. "We want to find that shortcut."

It turned out that Hendrick was the first to spot it. It was a narrow path, half hidden by chamisa, and sparsely traveled. They turned off and followed it, single file, as it led them gradually upward. It wasn't long before the scrubby piñons gave way to oaks and pines, and the air around them was pungent with pine scent. The needles rustled in the wind, making soft music that was pleasurable to the ear.

"It sure is nice up here," said Hendrick, glancing about. "Prettiest country I've ever seen."

The kid was a flatlander. Mountains were new to him. Probably he hadn't seen one before he got to New Mexico. Unless you counted the low-slung hills of the Ozarks, Cal had never seen real mountains before, either.

The sun was riding high when they stopped beside a rushing stream that was swollen with melted snow. They knelt and filled their canteens. Then they watered the animals.

"I'm more'n half starved," said Hendrick. "Can't we stay here long enough to fix something to eat?"

The kid was always hungry, but truth to tell, Cal could use some grub himself.

"All right, we'll stop. But we can't linger."

Cal built a small fire, encircled by fist-sized rocks. After they'd eaten and washed the meal down with coffee, they put out the fire and got under way. The fact that they'd both gone a long time with little sleep was finally taking its toll. He yearned to stay by that stream and take a nap.

"Do you think this trail is leading us in the right direction?" said Hendrick, when they'd left their campsite behind.

"That's what I was told by a man I trust. Why?"

"It doesn't seem like much, that's all. And there's nothing around us but trees."

"My friend knew what he was talking about. You're just going to have to trust me."

He was right about the trail not being much. It was so narrow at times that they were forced to ride single file. Branches encroached and had to be brushed aside.

"What was it you did, Thornton? Before you started chasing down outlaws, that is."

Cal saw no harm in satisfying the kid's curiosity. "I was in the Union Cavalry during what some call the 'Recent Unpleasantness.' I fought at Wilson's Creek in Missouri and Prairie Grove in Arkansas. After Lee surrendered, I got talked into pinning on a badge. I served for a while as a deputy in Linn County, Kansas, near the border. After that, I took to buying and selling. I'd buy things cheap when somebody was anxious to sell. Then I'd take whatever I'd bought someplace else where it was wanted or needed. I'd make a nice profit that way. At least most of the time."

"In other words, you were a peddler," said Hendrick.

"No," he said, disliking the term. "I was an opportunist. Some might even call me an entrepreneur."

"That's a funny sounding word. But whatever you call it, it sure beats working."

The kid had a lot of sass. Cal agreed that being a peddler beat the life of a soldier or a lawman, and it was certainly better than farming. Regardless of Hendrick's putdown, there was plenty of work and skill involved in trading. A good deal of risk went along with it too.

"Are you going back to what you used to do?" asked the kid. "When we finish this job, I mean."

Hendrick made it sound like the task of bringing a gang of outlaws to justice was going to be easy, and that it was certain they'd walk away and have a life of some kind afterward. It was plain that the kid didn't really understand what he was going to be up against, and this caused Cal another bout with guilt.

"I suppose I will go back to what I was doing," he said, in answer to the question. "Trading is a living, anyway. Worst that's ever happened is I got run out of town for selling a few cases of medicine that I'd bought from an actor. The members of the Ladies' Society all got drunk on that medicine. Dr. Buckles' Health Elixir, was what it was called. The ladies appeared to be having a good time, but their husbands and the local preacher weren't amused. The sheriff told me I'd better be long gone before those women sobered up and discovered what a hangover felt like. I figured he was right."

Hendrick chuckled. "I guess every job has its drawbacks. That Buckles fellow must have been a right fair doctor."

"More'n likely, he was a right fair moonshiner. Anyway, I fought shy of health elixirs after that close call."

"Did you try any of the stuff yourself?"

"No, I couldn't. I'd sold every last bottle. It hadn't occurred to me to sample it first."

A companionable silence fell between them, after that. When it was getting close to nightfall, they made camp in a shallow depression that gave them shelter from the cold wind and hid them from view of anyone coming up the trail. They bedded down, leaving the horses to warn of anyone's approach. Come daylight they continued along the narrow trail. Sunlight filtered through the needled branches, creating an eerie sense of otherworldliness. Maybe that was the cause of Cal's sense of foreboding. He tried to shake it off but couldn't. He had the uncanny feeling that his enemies from Las Vegas were following. What's more, he sensed that they were getting close.

"Are you all right?" asked Hendrick, suspecting something was wrong.

"I'm fine. It's just that I've got a hunch those three we left at the livery stable are catching up to us."

"What do you mean by 'hunch'?" he said, glancing uneasily over his shoulder.

"It's just a feeling, but when I get one, it's usually right."

Hendrick muttered a curse under his breath. "We don't need this. Not if we're going to overtake Pa's killers."

"Well, need it or not, we've got it to deal with."

The question now was, *how?*

Chapter Four

Cal's senses were alert as he led the way through the mountain forest. A feeling of danger wrapped itself around him. Still, there was no sign of the outlaws. When they paused for a breather, Hendrick voiced his concern.

"You're still worried, aren't you?"

Cal glanced back over the winding trail, though it wasn't possible to see very far.

"Yeah," he said. "I've learned to never ignore my hunches."

"What are we going to do?"

"I'm not sure, at least not yet. In the meantime, be ready."

As they rode on, Cal studied their situation. The more he thought about it, the clearer a course of action became. The only way to seize the advantage was to stop and face the enemy. But in order for this to work, he had to choose the right place to make a stand. What's more, he needed to find it soon. When he rounded a bend and saw a spill of boulders up ahead, he knew it was the place he'd been looking for.

"We'll stop there," he said, as they neared the fortress of stone.

Hendrick looked uneasy. "You're expecting a shoot-out, aren't you?"

Cal glanced at his stricken face. "I'm not going to lie to you. It's likely to come down to shooting. But the way I see it, it's better to fight face-to-face than to get shot in the back."

Hendrick fingered the grips of his newly acquired revolver. "I see your point," he said.

Cal dismounted and tethered Coronado and the zebra dun on a nearby patch of grass. Here, they were shielded from the trail. Hendrick secured the other animals close by. When this was done, they took positions behind the widest boulder.

"They couldn't have cut the lead we had on 'em this much, could they?" Hendrick asked, eyeing the empty trail.

It was wishful thinking.

"It's possible," he said. "In fact, it's probable. If my hunch is right, that's exactly what they did. Remember we made some stops to eat and sleep. But that outfit from Las Vegas is hopping mad. They won't have wasted any time. They'll stay on our trail and hunt us down like bloodhounds."

Hendrick looked downright sick. Cal wondered how he'd behave when the chips were down and lead was flying. He guessed that only time would tell.

Hendrick positioned the barrel of his rifle on the stone surface. Cal's own Winchester was propped nearby. As he looked back down the trail, every nerve in his body was taut and ready for action. But for the moment they were surrounded by a silence that was undisturbed, except for the wind-song in the pines and the raucous cry of a high flying crow. Cal imagined he could hear his own heartbeat.

Long minutes passed with nothing to disturb the peace of the forest. This was enough to satisfy Hendrick. He was ready to pull out for Santa Fe.

"I think you're jumping at shadows and imagining things," he accused.

"Maybe," said Cal, not wanting to argue even though he knew much better than his partner the nature of outlaws. "The way I see it, jumping at shadows is a whole lot better than ignoring the danger and getting killed."

Hendrick looked disgusted. "Since you're not going to listen to reason, I guess we'll have to wait and see who's right."

"I guess we will."

As the afternoon dragged on, the face of the boulder absorbed the sun's rays, radiating heat where Cal sat. He was sweating. A fly buzzed lazily around his nose. He took a swipe at the troublesome insect and missed. When he couldn't resist looking at his watch any longer, he pulled it from his vest and saw that only three-quarters of an hour had gone by since they'd stopped. It seemed twice as long.

Hendrick's impatience was palpable, making the wait even worse.

"Thornton, just what is it going to take to satisfy you that you're imagining things?" he said. His voice was an irritating whine.

Cal's jaw muscles tightened as he choked back a sharp reply.

"I'm not imagining things," he managed to say calmly. "We're staying right here until that gang shows up."

"But what about Barley and Santa Fe?"

"They'll keep. They'll have to. We've got this other job to take care of first."

"Well, if you're so sure they're coming, I wish they'd hurry up."

Hendrick got his wish. Not more than a minute passed before they heard a horse nicker in the distance.

Cal grabbed his rifle. "They're coming," he whispered anxiously.

"I heard."

Side by side, they stood waiting. Cal could hear a voice, now. It had the squeaky pitch of one of the three Las Vegas outlaws.

"You'd better not have guessed wrong, Coble," it said.

"I wasn't guessing. It was clear that they turned off the main trail and came this way. A greenhorn could have read the sign they left."

"Get ready," Cal whispered. "But don't shoot until I open the ball."

The first one to come into view was the big fellow. Squeaky Voice was next. When the third cleared the bend, Cal called out.

"Keep your hands where I can see 'em. Then climb down off your horses!"

The outlaws reined up. But instead of surrendering, they grabbed their guns.

"He's over there behind that big rock!" one of them shouted.

Bullets started flying and Cal was kept busy trying to hold them off. From what he could hear, Hendrick was doing his part, as well.

More than one bullet nicked the boulder, sending slivers of rock flying in every direction. One of the slivers plowed across the side of Cal's face, burning like the dickens as it went. He squeezed off a shot at his attacker. The outlaw fell from his saddle.

Hendrick's shots sent the other two scrambling for cover among the thickly needled pine branches. Their horses scattered and ran. Once the outlaws reached cover they released another barrage of gunfire. The air fogged up with thick acrid smoke. It was hard to breathe and right next to impossible to see. There was a lull in the shooting until a gust of wind swept down and blew the curtain of smoke away. Cal could see now. He spotted part of a blue shirt hidden among the low-slung branches. Getting a jump on the others, he aimed and fired. There was a cry of pain telling him he'd hit his target.

Away from cover, the unhorsed outlaw who'd opened the battle struggled to his knees. Cal spotted him as he was bringing up his pistol to fire. Without stopping to aim, Cal snapped off a shot. The outlaw fell backward. This time he wasn't getting up. Before Cal could turn his attention back to the pine-branch hideout, the shooting abruptly stopped.

"Are all of 'em dead?" said Hendrick, puzzled by the sudden cessation of gunfire.

"I don't think so. At least one of 'em's still alive. The

fellow who's with him might be as well, though I'm sure I wounded him."

"What do we do now?"

"Give whoever's left a chance to surrender."

The kid wiped sweat from his eyes and looked toward the pines.

"You, there, throw out your weapons!" Cal shouted. "Then come into the open and keep your hands where I can see 'em."

There was no answer.

"What now?" said Hendrick.

Cal's patience was at an end. "You, there, this is your last chance!"

"Hold your horses!" was the gruff reply. "Shorty's dead and I think you done killed Loftis too."

"Then drag the one that's with you out in the open where I can see him. Slide your guns out first."

The surviving outlaw surrendered his weapons and those of his partner. Then he dragged the body out onto the trail.

"Hendrick, keep him covered," Cal ordered as he pulled a leather strip from his pocket and started forward. One glance told him that Loftis was as dead as he was ever going to be. With the strip of leather, he bound the hands of the remaining gang member, the big bearlike one described to him. His bushy beard covered his face and he had long, tangled hair that fell down around his powerfully built shoulders. When he spoke, his voice was gruff.

"What's your name?" Cal asked.

The outlaw scowled. "Guess I don't mind telling you. I'm Barn Oak Phipps. Been called that for years 'cause

I'm tough as barn oak. The scrawny one over there is Shorty Coble. He don't look like much, but he's got a salty kinsman that's going to strip the hide off your back when he finds out you killed his cousin."

"I'm looking forward to meeting him," said Cal, his words dripping with sarcasm.

"I'll just bet you are. The other one you killed is Homer Loftis. Ole Homer, he fought with Captain Quantrill back along the Kansas border. He wasn't a fellow that you'd want to mess with, neither."

Well, he's not going to be a problem anymore. Cal had seen what Quantrill's bushwhackers had done to civilian populations. None of it nice. All of it barbaric. He felt no regret at having killed Loftis. None at all.

"It might be they're wanted," said Hendrick. "Maybe there's paper out on 'em offering a reward."

"Wouldn't surprise me a bit," said Cal.

"Let's tell the sheriff in Santa Fe. Then, if there's any money, we'll split it."

Cal pushed his hat to the back of his head and gave Hendrick a good long look. This was a side of the kid he hadn't expected.

"First off, we're not bounty hunters," he said. "More to the point, I don't want to tote their stinking bodies through the mountains, and I sure don't want to cut off their heads, which is another way the law identifies dead outlaws."

Hendrick backed off, looking a little sick. "Forget about it," he said.

Barn Oak appeared to be enjoying the kid's discomfiture. "Are you just going to leave 'em layin' there for the scavengers, sonny?"

"Why, I do believe you're a sensitive man, Barn Oak," said Cal.

The outlaw gave him a look that would scorch pancakes.

Cal went over to where the mules were picketed and pulled a shovel from one of the packs. When he got back, he dropped it in front of the remaining outlaw.

"I'm going to untie you so you can bury your dead," he said. "But I'm warning you, if you try anything funny, you're going to be joining the other two."

Phipps didn't like the prospect of hard physical labor, but he knew better than to open his mouth in protest.

"Hendrick, keep him covered," said Cal. "If you have to, shoot him."

Phipps bent over and grabbed the shovel, all the while muttering oaths under his breath. A short ways off the trail, he started digging. The rocky ground gave way with reluctance. He puffed and panted as he dug. Occasionally he paused to wipe sweat with a dirty-looking bandana. All the while Hendrick fidgeted, for he was anxious to get started again. At last a single grave was dug that was large enough to accommodate the remains of the dead outlaws. Cal ordered Phipps to tumble them in and cover them with dirt.

"Ain't you going to say any words over 'em?" he asked when the work was done. "It don't seem right not to."

"They were your friends," said Cal. "You can say whatever you want."

"Well, I can't seem to remember none," said Phipps, leaning heavily on the shovel. "Guess it don't make no difference nohow."

Cal wasn't surprised that he had no ready words to recite. He figured that Phipps was only stalling while he tried to think of a way to escape.

"I know some," Hendrick offered.

"Then go ahead," said Cal. "But don't take too long. Remember you're in a hurry to get to Santa Fe."

Hendrick cleared his throat. "I will sing of the mercies of the Lord forever . . ." he began.

Cal recognized it as a Psalm that Tate used to read. When Hendrick was finished, Cal tied the outlaw's hands again.

"You'd better do something to your face, Thornton," said his partner, seeming to notice the gash for the first time.

Cal put his hand to the place where the rock sliver had grazed him. It came away with a smear of blood.

"Just a scratch," he said, "but I'll clean it up and leave it to the open air to heal."

If it left a scar it wouldn't do anything for his looks, but then they weren't all that much to brag about in the first place. Rugged and masculine was what one attractive young lady had called them. Trying to be kind, no doubt.

When the wound was cleaned, he left Hendrick to guard the prisoner while he rounded up the outlaws' horses and gathered their weapons. Phipps claimed his own mount. The other horses were put on a lead. On the trail again, Cal went first, followed by Phipps. Hendrick came last with the animals so he could keep an eye on the prisoner. They'd lost a lot of daylight because of the long delay. When the sun dipped below the western horizon, they stopped and made camp in the shelter of the pines.

"Hendrick, you take the first watch," said Cal after they'd eaten a simple meal.

The kid gave him a look of surprise. "Why bother staying up all night? Phipps isn't going anywhere tied like that."

"But can you guarantee he's going to stay tied? Do you want to risk getting your throat cut in your sleep?"

Phipps roared with laughter. "Why, I do believe you're scair't of me," he taunted.

Cal ignored him. His problem right now was Hendrick. The kid wasn't convinced that the bushy-bearded, bearlike outlaw was still a danger.

"Look, you don't want to ruin your chance to get to Santa Fe, do you?"

"Uh, no, I reckon not."

"Then I suggest you take old Barn Oak here seriously."

Again, Phipps laughed.

Cal wasn't sure if he'd succeeded in convincing the boy of the danger. Still, Hendrick agreed to keep watch until midnight. At that time, Cal would take his place. Trusting the boy to do his job, he crawled between his blankets and dropped off to sleep.

He'd slept no more than a few hours before he was jolted awake by the sound of metal clanging against rock. Instinctively he grabbed for his gun. By the faint light of the moon he could see Phipps' silhouette bending over Hendrick's prone body. The outlaw was reaching for the Colt that Cal had confiscated back in Las Vegas.

"Hold it right there, Phipps!" he ordered.

Surprised, the big man drew back.

"Are you all right, Hendrick?" he called as he kicked himself free from his bedding.

The kid moaned and struggled to sit up. "That no-account threw the coffee pot and hit me in the head. Must have knocked me out for a minute."

The clanging sound that Cal heard was the pot ricocheting off a low rock overhang. Good thing for the alarm, or else they'd both be dead.

"Cover him, Hendrick, while I tie him up again."

Phipps cursed as a new rawhide strip went around his wrists. When he was secured, Cal took the added precaution of tying him to a tree trunk with a length of rope.

"Young whelp was sound asleep," said Phipps. "He was snoring like all get out. I almost had him. He deserved a conk on the head."

Cal wasn't inclined to disagree. Hendrick had come close to getting them both killed.

"Sorry I let you down," said Hendrick, gently touching the knot that had risen on his head.

"It was my fault," said Cal. "I should have taken the first watch and let you get some sleep. I hope you've learned to keep your guard up around outlaws."

"I've learned," he said ruefully.

Cal took the watch for the rest of the night. He moved a good distance away from where Phipps was tied. This was in case he nodded off the way Hendrick had done. He didn't want the outlaw to know it. Sometime later, Cal did doze off.

He woke with a start to find it was daylight. A mountain jay landed on a nearby branch, its bright blue feathers a contrast to the green needles. The air was fresh and the wilderness pristine. The kid was still asleep. From the sound of it, so was Phipps. The realization came to him that the Las Vegas gang would trouble him no more. For the first time in a long while Cal felt good about the way things were going.

He put the dented coffeepot over the fire, and soon the aroma of Arbuckle's Best was sending a wake-up message to the others. They ate. Then they broke camp and headed out. This time they didn't have to worry about being hunted. Once again, they were the hunters.

"I do believe you fellas have gone and got yourselves lost," said Phipps, when they'd been on the trail for an hour or so. "Why, you're going to wander through these mountains for weeks. Likely, you'll never find your way out and you'll starve to death." He shook with laughter then, like he'd told a funny joke.

"Is he right?" Hendrick demanded to know. "Are we lost like he says?"

Cal was annoyed by Phipps' tactic of playing on Hendrick's gullibility and undermining his confidence.

"Stay calm," he said. "Barn Oak here is simply trying to worry you, is all. So long as we stick to the trail, we're going to come out all right."

It was plain that the kid wasn't convinced. Still, having no choice, he followed along.

By afternoon, they were on their way down the slope. When they reached the bottom, they could see Santa Fe in the distance.

"Get a move on, Phipps," Cal ordered. "We've found our way off the mountain and now we've got to find you a nice safe place to spend the night."

With a jail cell looming in his immediate future, the outlaw favored them with a few colorful phrases that he'd overlooked before.

When they rode into town, Cal kept a look out for five men fitting the killers' descriptions. The streets were made of nothing but dirt that a brisk wind constantly re-arranged. The mud-colored buildings sat side by side, each a copy of all the others. As they entered a street that led to the plaza, they were greeted by the pungent smells of cattle and horse droppings. Anyone expecting to find an impressive city was sure to be disappointed. Still, the place was bustling. It remained the western ter-minus of the commerce trail, though that fortune maker wasn't apt to be in use much longer, thanks to the en-croaching railroads. When he reached the square, Cal stopped and spoke to a hefty-looking fellow who was unloading bags of grain from a wagon.

"Can you tell us where the sheriff's office is?" he asked.

"That way," said the man, pointing to a side street that led north.

It turned out that the jail was adobe, like every other building in town. The sheriff, who introduced himself as Randolph, took a disgruntled Phipps off their hands. When the outlaw was safely locked up, Randolph in-vited them to sit and drink coffee while they told their story. When Cal was finished, Randolph leafed through his stack of wanted dodgers.

"Here he is," he said. "Ezra 'Barn Oak' Phipps, wanted

for bank robbery. There's a three-hundred-dollar reward for his capture."

"What about the others?" said Hendrick, hopeful of getting more money.

Randolph shuffled through papers again and pulled out two more dodgers. "Both of 'em are wanted," he said. "Coble, for a couple of bank robberies and one murder. Loftis, pretty much the same, except he has two notches on his gun. Each one of 'em has four hundred dollars on his head."

"Well, we got both of 'em," said Hendrick. "We buried 'em on the mountain. Don't we get the eight-hundred-dollar reward?"

Randolph looked regretful. "Sorry son, but without proof there's no way that I can put in a claim."

Hendrick glared at Cal. "I told you we should have brought their bodies in."

Cal made it a point to ignore him.

"We're not bounty hunters," he told the sheriff. "I'm not lugging around a couple of bodies no matter how much the reward."

"I understand," said Randolph. "I can write you a three-hundred-dollar bank draft for bringing Phipps in. They'll reimburse me. You're welcome to their horses and gear, as well. Take 'em down to Abner Watts at the trading post. I'll give you a note saying it's all right for you to sell them. He'll give you a fair price."

While the sheriff scribbled a note, Cal downed the last of his coffee. Then he got up, took the note and the bank draft, and shook Randolph's hand.

"Thanks," he said. "We'll be on our way, now. You be sure and take good care of Barn Oak for us."

"Will do," said Randolph. "That fellow's not going anywhere."

"Oh, one more thing, Sheriff. We're on the trail of a bunch of outlaws who killed a friend of mine, as well as Hendrick's father. The leader is a big fellow named Barley. Another one's called McGill. They were supposed to be coming to Santa Fe to find someone. Would you be able to tell me anything about them?"

Randolph nodded. "Yeah, I know of Barley and his outfit, but I heard they'd gone east."

"Well, they're back. Guess I'll have to ask around."

Randolph went over and looked out the front window. "If you need a place to start, I'd advise you stop in at Señorita Lucinda Martinez's cantina. It's down that street and to the right. She took over the place after her father died. She's a smart lady, and very little happens in Santa Fe that Señorita Martinez doesn't know about."

"Thanks. I'll stop and have a word with her."

"I wish you good hunting," said Randolph.

When they got to the trading post, Hendrick was still sulking about the lost reward money. He stayed in the background, something that Cal didn't mind at all. Abner Watts, a narrow-faced man with shrewd eyes, read the sheriff's note.

"I'll give you a good deal," he said, "seeing as how the sheriff thinks highly of what you've done."

The sale of the three horses, two saddles that were in good shape, and the various pistols and rifles brought another three hundred dollars. The only things Cal kept back were the Colt .44 that he'd given to Hendrick and a fancy, almost-new saddle which he was loathe to turn loose.

Their next stop was the bank, where he cashed the draft while the kid waited outside. He came out and slipped him a roll of bills.

"Here's your half of the six hundred dollars," he said.

Hendrick looked surprised as he took the money. "Thanks. I'm ashamed to admit it, but I guess I never really expected you to split it with me."

"You did half the capturing and took half the risk. Why not?"

The roll of bills, along with Cal's acknowledgment of the part he'd played, took away the sulks. Hendrick started looking downright cheerful.

"I'd advise you to put that money away and not let anyone see it," said Cal. "When this is over you'll want to make something of yourself. Whatever it is you decide to do, three hundred dollars will come in handy."

He watched the kid tuck the money inside his shirt. *Thornton, you ought to take your own advice,* he thought. *What have you made of yourself? You haven't invested in anything, or planted crops, or tried to better yourself. All you've done is live from one day to another, wandering over Kansas, making a living by your wits.*

"It's strange," said Hendrick, "but I haven't been able to think past catching up with those killers. I know Pa wanted me to be a man who folks respected. But I don't know what to do to make that happen."

The kid surprised him. He was thinking in a mature way.

"I'm afraid that nobody can tell you," said Cal, remembering the pain of his own youthful confusion. "This is something you've got to figure out by yourself."

He sometimes wished he had one of those fortune-teller's glass balls that would show him the future. But then again, maybe he didn't want to see down the road that lay before him. If somebody was to calculate the odds of him and the kid surviving, he was sure they wouldn't be good. *No, best to deal with the future as it unwinds.* Even if he wasn't able to figure a way to beat the odds, he couldn't turn back. He'd made a vow to the best friend he'd ever had. He intended to keep it.

Chapter Five

The cantina was located a short distance off the plaza.
Its size equaled three of the other buildings put together.

"You think this woman can help us?" said Hendrick,
as they hitched their animals to the post in front.

"Randolph seems to think so. It's worth a try, anyway."

Cal entered first. Inside the doorway he paused to give
his eyes a chance to adjust to the dim interior. Lively music issued from a far corner where a fellow sat plucking
guitar strings in a rapid rhythm.

He spotted an empty table and led the way. There, he
seated himself so he could see the entire room. Hendrick took the chair to his right.

The cantina was more than half full. The patrons
were a mix of both Mexicans and Anglos. A couple of
lovely señoritas were serving the food and exchanging
light banter with customers, both in Spanish and English. They wore ankle-length skirts in bright colors,

along with embroidered tops. Silver dangled from their ears. Hendrick had never seen the like before. They had his full attention. Cal wondered which one was Señorita Martinez, but he wasn't surprised to find that she was neither. Before they could order, an elegant-looking young woman approached their table. Her hair was drawn back, emphasizing her fine features. The light-gray dress she wore was simple, but it was clearly new and costly.

"You are Señor Thornton, are you not?" she asked, her voice modulated, her English perfect.

He stood, as did Hendrick. "Yes," he acknowledged and introduced his partner.

"Please be seated, gentlemen," she said, as she took the chair across from them. "Sheriff Randolph sent word to me of your mission. He thought I might be of some small assistance."

"Then I guess he told you we're going after the Barley gang."

"Yes, but I'm afraid you are too late to catch them here. My sources tell me they left this morning shortly after sunrise."

The news hit him like a bucket of cold water. The shortcut through the mountains hadn't been enough.

"They were coming here to find someone," he said. "Would you know if they did? And can you tell me who it was?"

Her expression was one of regret. "No, I'm sorry. They were only here for a brief time. Perhaps they failed to find the one they were seeking and went on without him. I'm told there were five when they departed the city, the same five who rode in."

Señorita Martinez appeared to have dependable sources of information.

"You wouldn't have any idea where it was they were headed?"

"Only that they mentioned in the hearing of one of my employees that they were going north. Also that it was important business they were on. Isobel got the impression their destination was Taos."

At least he had that. He wondered if he should pay her for the information she'd given him. She appeared to read his thoughts.

"No," she said. "Don't even consider payment. I do this because I despise men like Barley, and all those who ride with him. If you should kill him, you will be doing the Territory of New Mexico a favor."

As she spoke of Barley, her expression turned suddenly fierce. It was clear that Señorita Martinez was a woman you didn't want to cross.

"Then I will only say *gracias,* Señorita."

She smiled then. " 'Thank you' is enough. Now, I will send Luz to serve you. I wish you Godspeed."

Gracefully she rose from her chair, sweeping her skirts to the side. Cal watched her walk away with all the dignity and grace of a young queen.

"She's really beautiful," whispered Hendrick.

"Powerful too, I would wager. At least here in Santa Fe."

Luz came to their table to take their order. She was pretty and vivacious. When she asked Hendrick what he wanted, his face flushed and he acted tongue-tied. Cal had to order for both of them. Luz hurried off, leaving behind a vague scent of flowers.

When she returned with their meal, Hendrick kept stealing glances at her. Cal was amused that something could take the kid's attention away from food. Luz was attractive, but it was her employer who would turn the most heads.

By the time they left the cantina it was dark and they needed to find a place to stay the night. Cal was wary as they rode down the street. More than one person knew he was carrying a large sum of money. He stopped at the livery stable they'd passed on their way into town. For a few dollars they got the horses and mules fed and a place to sleep. Cal slept lightly, his hand near his gun.

The first rays of light were trailing across his blankets when he woke with a start. It took a moment to recall where he was. He pulled on his boots and nudged Hendrick awake.

"Get your horse saddled and your gear packed," he said. "We're heading for Taos."

After the customary grumbling, the kid was on his feet and ready to find something to eat. After a hurried meal, they headed out.

With Santa Fe behind them, Cal wondered about Barley's reason for going there. *Who was it he was supposed to have met? Why was this person so important?*

The sun was rising on the eastern horizon when he spotted a cluster of buildings in the distance. They looked like a kind of fungus that had grown on the surface of the land. At the largest of the structures, horses were hitched to the rail.

"Is that a ranch?" Hendrick wondered aloud.

"More likely it's a tavern or a way station."

"Are we going to stop there?"

"Yes, but don't let your guard down. Barley and his outfit might be inside. If they are, don't let on that you recognize them, and don't start anything."

"I won't," he promised. "I kinda hope it's them. Not being able to do anything but follow them from here to yonder starts to wear on a person."

"I reckon you can stand up under it for a while longer."

They reined up at the hitch rail and climbed down. Three horses were already tied there. Since the Barley gang had stolen three horses and a mule from Tate and a horse from the elder Hendrick, in addition to the five they started out with, he doubted they were the ones inside. At least not all of them were.

"Let's go," he said. "And let me do the talking."

Hendrick hung back while Cal took the lead. The place was, as he'd guessed, a tavern, albeit a crude one. Planks had been laid across barrels to form the bar. Behind it, shelves were nailed to the wall to hold a mismatched assortment of glassware. Beside the shelves, a door led to a back room. Three tables, each different from the others, took up most of the space on the front side of the bar. One of them was occupied by the owners of the horses. They were a rough-looking trio by anyone's standards. Cal noticed the bartender was keeping a wary eye on them. He was a man who enjoyed his meals, by the looks of him, but he wasn't soft by any means. Cal judged him to be on the far side of forty, maybe even older than fifty. His face was partly covered by a fulsome mustache and a pair of bushy "burnsides" that served to emphasize his drooping jowls.

"Come on in, gents," he invited, seeming glad of their arrival. "What'll you have?"

"What have you got?" Cal responded. "We're both hungry as wolves."

"There's some stew on the fire and a pot of strong, hot coffee. Fact is, if you want something stronger, you'll have to order whiskey."

"The stew and coffee will be fine," he said, aware that the three men at the other table were sizing him up. Not being a trusting fellow, he took a chair at an empty table that faced the room. Hendrick had sense enough to take the seat to his left, giving them both a clear view of the trio.

"Hurry up, Dollarhide!" one of them ordered rudely. "My glass is empty and I want more of that mess you call stew." To Cal's way of thinking, he had the look of a pirate. He spoke with a French accent.

"Keep your britches on, Frenchie," said Dollarhide. "I've got other folks to wait on besides you. When I'm finished, you're next."

"Settle down, Ledoux," said one of his companions. "Old Dollarhide ain't scared of you."

"Shut up, Coble," he said, glaring at everyone.

Dollarhide ducked into the back room and reappeared again with a shotgun in his hand.

"Any of you gents want to start trouble?" he said.

Cal's estimate of the tavern keeper went way up. Dollarhide had sand.

It was clear by Ledoux's surprised look that he'd

gotten more than he'd bargained for. Coble jumped to his feet, not liking this new turn of events.

"You'd better watch yourself, old man," he threatened. "We might come back here when you're all by your lonesome and burn this place down."

"Try it," said Dollarhide, "and I'll be leaving you for the buzzards to feast on."

"Come on, Marsh," said Ledoux. "Coble, you too. Let's get out of here."

While Marsh and Ledoux headed for the door, Coble stood his ground.

"We've got lots of friends," he said, "and they'd be glad to help us teach you some respect."

"Bring 'em with you," said Dollarhide. "This here greener can take 'em all on."

Cal's fingers inched toward the .44 at his side. He saw that Hendrick was ready too. Coble glanced over, adding them both to the fact that Dollarhide was well armed with a shotgun that could do a lot of damage. He didn't like the sum. Warily he backed toward the door that the others had exited. Cal listened as they rode away.

"I'm sure glad you gents stopped by," said Dollarhide. "Those three were getting to be a nuisance."

Cal chuckled. "Looks to me like you took care of things just fine."

"With the help of this here greener."

"But aren't you afraid they'll come back and burn your place down, Mr. Dollarhide?" said Hendrick.

"They might try it, son, but I'll be ready for 'em. Anyway, I expect that Coble fellow was just letting off some steam. Now to get you fed."

He went to the back room and brought out two bowls of stew. Next came cups of black coffee. While they were eating, the tavern owner sat down at the other table facing them

"If you fellows are going north, you'd best watch out that they don't ambush you."

"North is where we're headed," said Cal. "We're after an outfit that's a lot like the three you ran off. There's five of 'em, though. Back in Kansas they killed a friend of mine and the boy's pa."

Dollarhide scratched his chin in thought. "Sounds like you might be talking about Matt Barley and the no-account heathens that ride with him. They stopped by here this morning. Didn't stay long, though. Acted like they were expected someplace. Another fella came along too, not long after they left. A Mexican fella. Nice and polite. Asked a few questions, but he didn't stay long, either. I'd have swore he was trailing 'em."

Cal wondered if Señorita Martinez had sent a man to follow the gang. She hadn't said anything about having done so, but she was clearly a woman who kept her own counsel. It might be that this man was acting as her spy.

"They didn't mention anything about Taos, did they?" said Hendrick.

Dollarhide shrugged. "Not that I recollect. But they sure enough were headed in that direction. I watched 'em ride out. Needed to make sure that they didn't take what wasn't theirs."

The room was now in semidarkness. The barkeep got up took a lamp from a shelf and set it on one of the tables. Fumbling a little, he took the mantle off and touched a match to the wick. A flame leapt up and bathed the room in soft light. Cal watched shadows shoot across the wall.

"That's better," said Dollarhide, replacing the glass. "Are you fellows planning on riding out tonight?"

"Not if you've got a place where we can bed down," said Cal.

"There's a room next to this one. It's got bunks in it, and I'd be pleased if you'd stay. No charge. This is one night I'd welcome some company, just in case they do decide to turn back."

Cal guessed that the tavern owner was a lot more worried than he'd let on.

"We're obliged," he said. "Now, I'm going out to take care of the horses and mules. I'd like to turn them into the corral, if that's all right."

"Fine with me," said their host.

Hendrick followed Cal outside. They worked together under the starlit sky.

When they were finished and starting for the tavern, Hendrick hung back.

"Something wrong?" asked Cal.

"Do you think those men will come back here and cause trouble tonight?"

"I doubt it," said Cal, hoping he was right. "You see, Dollarhide isn't alone anymore, and he's a salty old man. If they cause trouble, we can give it back to them. Coble and his friends are the kind that like the deck stacked in their favor."

Back inside, Dollarhide showed them to their bunks. Sleeping in a bed was a pleasant change after all those nights spent on the ground or in a hayloft. It didn't take Cal long to drop off.

The aroma of coffee woke him. Dollarhide had a breakfast of eggs and bacon waiting. Hendrick didn't waste any time doing the meal justice. For that matter, neither did Cal.

"We thank you for your hospitality," he told the tavern keeper when they were ready to leave.

"You did me a good turn by being here," said Dollarhide. "Consider us even."

They saddled two of their horses, put the others and the mules on a lead rope, and headed north.

"Those fellows left an easy trail to follow," Hendrick observed, as he leaned over for a closer look. "It appears they're going in the same direction as the Barley gang."

"Noticed that, did you?" said Cal. "I'm betting they're all headed straight for the same place."

Hendrick eased back in the saddle. "Now, what do you suppose is going on?"

He was wondering that himself. "I don't know," he said, "but I'm sure going to try to find out."

As they made their way northward, Cal realized that his thinking had changed. In the beginning, all he wanted to do was avenge Tate's murder. Now he was faced with a puzzle, one with some of the pieces missing.

They were well away from Dollarhide's tavern when they spotted a man up ahead. He was on foot, but just barely. As they watched, he staggered and nearly fell.

"That fella must be crazy," said Hendrick. "Dollarhide's is the closest place."

"I doubt he's on foot by choice. He might be the man

that Dollarhide told us about. The Señorita may have sent him."

He spotted them and waved to get their attention. Cal nudged Coronado in the sides and galloped toward him. Hendrick followed on the gray.

When they reined up in front of the man, he had his hat in his hand. There was a cut on his scalp and a large knot had risen. It was plain that his head had recently connected with something hard.

"My friend, it looks like you've had some trouble," said Cal.

"*Sí*, Señor. I will tell you my story, but do you have some water you can spare?"

Cal loosened the canteen and handed it down to him.

"*Gracias*," he said, and tipped it up to swallow.

The man was young, certainly no older than Cal. He was lean and work-hardened and he might well have been a cousin or brother of Señorita Martinez.

"Was it three hombres that did this to you?"

The stranger returned the canteen. "*Sí*, they came upon my camp while I was sleeping. I fought back, but one of them hit me on the head. When I recovered my senses, my rifle and pistol were gone. So were my horse and my gear."

"We're on the trail of five killers," said Cal. "Those three you tangled with are headed in the same direction."

"Would one of the men you are seeking go by the name of Barley?"

Maybe Cal should have been surprised, but he wasn't. Barley seemed to be cutting a wide swath here in the Territory.

"Yes," he admitted. "What do you know about him?"

"First, permit me to introduce myself. I am Emilio Garcia of Galisteo. I was on my way to the Carroway ranch where my sister works. She sent word by a man who was fired that both she and the owners are in trouble."

"In what way?" asked Hendrick.

"The foreman has taken over the place. My sister, Lucinda, is a virtual prisoner, along with the rancher and his niece. In her message she said that the foreman, a man named Pete Jared, had sent for an outlaw called Barley to come and help him."

So this is what it's all about, thought Cal.

"My name's Cal Thornton," he said. "This tall, skinny fellow beside me is Ross Hendrick. We can loan you a horse since we're all going in the same direction."

"I would be much obliged. I am very worried."

Cal was glad that he'd kept the outlaw's fancy saddle. Garcia was a little unsteady on his feet, but he managed to mount one of the spare horses without assistance.

"Ready to ride?" said Hendrick, who clearly doubted Garcia's ability to do so.

"I am," he replied. "Although I will be of little use since I have no gun. The outlaws stole everything but my boots."

Cal regretted not keeping another of the outlaws' pistols. But that train had already left the station, as Tate used to say.

The rising wind was playing havoc with the loose soil. The tracks they followed were filling in quickly. Cal nudged Coronado to get him moving. There was plenty of room to ride side by side. He and Hendrick kept Garcia between them.

"I trust you know how to get to this Carroway ranch," said Cal.

"*Sí,* the ranch hand who brought Lucinda's message gave me the directions. Before we get to Taos, we must turn east and go through the canyon and into the mountains. The ranch is located in a high valley on the other side."

"Sounds like the place is way off in the middle of nowhere," said Hendrick.

"True," said Garcia. "It makes a perfect place for harboring outlaws who are on the run from the law and are willing to pay a great deal of money for a hideout."

A good setup, thought Cal. *This Jared fellow had come up with quite a scheme. But what of the owner of the ranch, his niece, and Garcia's sister? They'd simply be in the way. Outlaws like Barley were quick to deal with anyone who got in their way. The Carroways' days were surely numbered. So were those of Señorita Garcia.*

"We can't afford to waste any time," said Cal, knowing that Garcia was well aware of the danger to his sister.

"On that matter, we agree, *mi* amigos," he said.

They quickened their pace to match the urgency of the situation. When they stopped for a breather, Hendrick asked about Coble.

"I've been wondering about something. Since he's got the same name as the outlaw you shot on the mountain, do you suppose they're related somehow? Could he be the kinsman who Barn Oak Phipps mentioned?"

"I'd say he's the same kind of man Phipps described," said Cal. "It's a fair bet that he's the man we were warned about."

"Then I guess it's a good thing ole Barn Oak is locked up in a Santa Fe hoosegow, else he'd be finding Coble and putting him onto us."

"What's this about Barn Oak?" said Garcia.

Hendrick told the story of why they'd left Kansas and what had happened to them in Las Vegas and later in the mountains.

"It appears that you've had some difficulties since leaving Kansas," said Garcia.

An understatement, thought Cal.

The miles passed. Somehow Garcia managed to stay in the saddle. No doubt he felt pain from the blow he'd been dealt. But he was game. It was plain he was worried about his sister. The way Cal had the situation sized up, he had every right to be.

Chapter Six

Two nights later they were camped in a canyon with steep wooded sides. The knot had gone down on Garcia's head, and he was looking better. He lay back, resting against his grounded saddle.

"What good am I without a gun?" he bemoaned. "All I can do is fight with my fists or maybe throw sticks and stones at the outlaws. They even took away my knife."

Hendrick sympathized with his feeling of helplessness. "Look, Thornton gave me a .44 that he took from an outlaw, so you're welcome to use my rifle."

"*Gracias,*" he said. "My sister should never have gone off to that remote place to work for strangers. But the Carroway woman persuaded her, wanting her company, and Lucinda was always strong willed. When she made up her mind to do something, she wouldn't let anyone persuade her otherwise."

"Don't worry, we'll get her out of there," said Cal, sounding a lot more certain than he actually felt.

He moved away from the others and the warmth of

the campfire, and spread his blankets in the darkness. Caution had become a habit. As he lay there, he thought about the way things had gone. He acknowledged that he'd changed. When he'd ridden away from Tate's soddy, the only thing on his mind had been vengeance. That—or justice—was still what he was after, only now there was more at stake. *A lot more*. Not only was he responsible for the life and safety of a greenhorn kid, he had to find a way to rescue two women and an old man. His relatively carefree days as a traveling trader seemed far away. The others had fallen asleep and the fire had shrunk to a few small embers before he dropped off himself.

At daybreak, they broke camp. The trail they followed led them deeper through the canyon. A red-tailed hawk appeared in the sky and swooped down to look them over. Satisfied that they were of no further interest, it soared away on an updraft. Cal envied the bird's grace and freedom of flight.

Soon the trail was leading them into the mountains. The fragrant pines of the canyon slopes gave way to tall spruces and copses of aspens. The air was even lighter here. It was a beautiful place. Cal was struck by the irony that this peaceful land was also dangerous.

When they arrived at an overlook the following day, Cal pulled a pair of field glasses from his pack. Leaving the others behind, he crawled to the edge. When he looked through the glasses, he viewed a wide valley that was surrounded by mountains. On the near side stood a large house built from logs. Someone had planted lilac bushes in front and they were in bloom. A short distance from the house stood a barn, a corral, a structure that looked like a bunk house, and another that was probably a mess hall. There were some smaller outbuildings, as well. The place had an air of prosperity about it.

There were four men moving around near the corral and barn. The corral was filled with horses. No doubt some of them were Tate's. He looked toward the house and saw that all was quiet there. A lone man lounged near the door, smoking a cigarette. *He's probably guarding the Carroways,* Cal thought.

"May I have a look?" said Garcia, who'd crawled up beside him.

Cal handed the field glasses over. "Shade the lenses so they don't reflect," he cautioned. "I'd just as soon they weren't tipped off that we're up here."

Garcia was quiet as he looked the ranch over.

"It is as I feared," he said, handing the glasses back. "The outlaws have gathered."

"What are we going to do about it?" said Hendrick, who was standing back away from the edge, holding the mules and the horses.

Cal crawled away from the ledge before standing up. "My friend, I need you to stay here and take charge of the animals and our supplies. Garcia and I are going down there to see if we can get hired on."

Hendrick's jaw dropped in surprise. "You're not serious," he said.

"As serious as I can be. Now, Garcia will need to borrow your pistol. If you have any trouble up here, use the rifle."

Cal expected rebellion on Hendrick's part. Instead, he unbuckled his gun belt and handed it over. Garcia hesitated before taking it.

"Are you sure?" he said. "I am asking much of you."

"Yeah," said Hendrick. "I'm sure."

Cal felt a grudging sense of pride in the boy. He was maturing.

Garcia fastened the belt around his waist. "*Gracias,* amigo," he murmured.

Hendrick turned to Cal then. "I don't see how you're going to be able to do this. I mean, how can you go down there and work alongside the men who murdered your friend? I couldn't do it and that's a fact."

Hendrick had a point. This wasn't going to be an easy thing for him to do. He wanted to see every last one of Tate's killers hanged or shot. If he got hired, he'd be tempted to draw his gun and shoot as many as he could before they cut him down. There were also the prisoners to think about, and infiltrating the gang appeared to be the only way to rescue them.

"Look, I'll do whatever I have to," he said. "If you can think of another way, now is the time to speak up."

Hendrick was silent, but only for a moment.

"Think about it, Thornton, if the ones who robbed Garcia are down there, won't they recognize him?"

"Oh, I do not think so," said Garcia. "It was much too dark. They couldn't have gotten a good look at my face, if they got a look at all. Besides, I was alone then. They won't expect the man they assaulted to have a partner. And since they took my weapons, they won't suspect a man who is armed."

Hendrick didn't look like he was entirely convinced, but he kept his misgivings to himself.

"We've got to get on down there," said Cal. He handed the field glasses to Hendrick. "Here, you take these.

Keep an eye on the place. If we don't come back within a reasonable amount of time, ride to Taos. Get the word out about what's happening here. Make sure they know that two women are in trouble at the Carroway ranch."

"I'll do it," he promised. "But you take care and come back in one piece."

"That's my intention," said Cal.

Leaving Hendrick behind, they wended their way down the mountainside. Cal was riding Coronado; Garcia, the zebra dun. At last, they reached the valley floor. They were approaching the ranch buildings when two men rode out to intercept them.

"Steady," Cal cautioned. "I expect they just want to look us over. Maybe bully us a little."

Garcia nodded. His expression was resolute.

One member of the welcoming committee fit the hostler's description of the scrawny McGill. The other was the Frenchman from Dollarhide's place. In a minute they'd know if he and Garcia would pass the test.

"Hold up there!" McGill ordered. "You hombres are trespassing on private land."

Cal reined in Coronado and waited for McGill and his partner to get closer.

"Trespassing?" he said. "Well, we sure don't mean to be. Me and my pard here are looking for jobs, is all. Thought maybe you could use some help."

"I've seen you," said the Frenchman, glaring at Cal. "You and a kid were at that tavern Dollarhide runs."

"Yep," Cal admitted. "You saw us all right."

"What happened to the kid?"

Cal had a story ready. "Seems he had friends in Taos, so we parted company. Garcia here rode down to join me."

Ledoux was clearly suspicious. McGill was down-right hostile. This wasn't going well. The revolver on Cal's hip felt heavier all of a sudden.

While the two sides were taking each other's measure, another man rode up and joined them. His clothes were almost new and obviously expensive. The horse that he rode was a fine one. No doubt it was the best from the corral. Cal wondered if it might not have belonged to Tate, who'd had a good eye for horseflesh. The newcomer was arrogant in expression and manner, alerting everyone that he considered himself to be a cut above. Cal guessed he was the foreman, Pete Jared.

"What's going on here?" Jared demanded to know. "Who are these men?"

"We're trying to rustle up jobs," said Cal. "Figured you might be able to use a couple of extra hands."

From Jared's expression, hiring them was the last thing he wanted to do. Still, he was curious about them showing up on the out-of-the-way Carroway ranch without warning.

"Where have you worked?" he asked, digging for information.

"Here and there," said Cal. "Texas, Kansas, some in Colorado."

"And you?" he said, turning his attention to Garcia.

"I am from Socorro. I've worked in that area as well as Colorado. It was north of here that I met my friend Thornton."

"If you're partners," said Ledoux, "then why weren't you both at Dollarhide's?"

Cal hoped that Garcia was a good liar.

"I waited outside, hidden, until you left the tavern. I

didn't know who you were. For all I knew, you carried badges. A man can't be too careful."

Good for you, thought Cal. It was a reasonable explanation and it sent the message that Garcia was wanted. With luck, this would ease their suspicions a little.

Jared appeared to come to a decision. "Very well," he said, "if you're not afraid of work and if you can do what you're told, you're hired."

McGill scowled. Clearly he didn't approve of what Jared had done, yet he wasn't prepared to countermand his order. Ledoux seemed to lose interest all of a sudden. He wheeled his mount and rode off.

"We need a couple of new outhouses," said Jared. "Report to Buck Hogue. He'll hand you pickaxes and shovels and tell you where to dig."

"Barley isn't going to like this," said McGill, who couldn't hold his tongue any longer.

Jared glared at him. "Do you think I give a rat's backside what Barley likes or dislikes? The man works for me. He doesn't give the orders around here."

Cal had no idea which of the outlaws was Buck Hogue or where to find him. Still, he didn't want to ask McGill; and Jared, considering the matter finished, was leaving.

"Well, don't just sit there looking dumb," said McGill. "Hogue's over at the cook-shack riding herd on Wren."

He pointed to an outbuilding attached to what must have been the mess hall. Smoke was rising from a stovepipe, only to get blown away by the wind. Cal nudged Coronado forward. Garcia followed.

When they got there, a heated discussion was taking place inside the shack. Cal opened the door a crack and looked inside. A big man, fully six feet tall with a lot of bulk, was squared off against a fellow who could have passed for a leprechaun. The difference between the two in size and appearance was so incongruous as to be funny. The big man had to be Hogue, who was certainly one of Tate's killers. The leprechaun had a thatch of sandy-colored hair and a small, neat mustache. His eyes were bright with anger. Even though the top of his head barely reached Hogue's chest, he appeared to be holding his own in the verbal sparring.

Cal swung the door open wide, and he and Garcia stepped inside the small room. Hogue spun around, his face red with rage. He had to be one of the big men who the Las Vegas hostler had described when questioned about Tate's killers.

"Just who are you two, and what are you doing here?" he demanded to know.

Cal's hand itched to draw on the killer. He was so mad he couldn't find his voice. It was Garcia who spoke up.

"Mr. Jared hired us and sent us to you. You're supposed to put us to work doing some digging."

He sized them up, taking a good look at their side arms. "Digging for what?" he asked. "Gold?"

"Mr. Jared mentioned something about outhouses."

Hogue's hostility turned to amusement. "He did, did he? Well, come along then. I recall there's a couple of shovels and a pickaxe in the shed. I'll show you where to dig."

"We've got to take care of our horses first," said Cal.

"Don't bother. Green can do it." He went to the door and whistled over another outlaw. It turned out to be the young, mean-looking one.

"Go feed those two horses," he said, indicating Coronado and the zebra dun that Garcia had borrowed from Cal. "Take off their gear and rub 'em both down. Then turn 'em into the corral."

Green was only a few years older than Hendrick, but anyone could tell at a glance that he was dangerous. It was apparent in his eyes. He was the kind who went around looking for trouble, and when he couldn't find it, he did his best to stir it up. He made it plain that he resented Hogue's orders.

"Don't you think I've got better things to do than nursemaid a couple of nags?" he said. "Besides, you're not my boss."

"Jared's orders," said Hogue, his eyes narrowing to slits. "If you don't like 'em, then take it up with Jared, or with Barley."

At the mention of Barley's name, Green gave Hogue a look that would've scorched the tail off a scorpion. He muttered a curse before stepping over and grabbing the reins of Coronado and the zebra dun. He was still cursing as he walked off toward the stable.

"Young donkey," said Hogue, when he was sure that Green was out of earshot. "I'm going to teach him a lesson one of these days. But now it's time for you two saddle bums to get to work."

They were handed shovels and a couple of pickaxes. Then Hogue led them to the place where they were to dig. He stood watching as Cal and Garcia took turns breaking into the hard ground. Finally, he got bored and wandered off.

"Well, what do you think?" said Garcia, after Hogue had gone.

"I think we've landed in a nest of vipers."

"They don't seem to like one another much, either. Have you noticed the discord?"

"Couldn't help it. I think that mutual greed is all that's keeping this bunch together."

Garcia glanced toward the house. "I must find a way to talk to Lucinda."

"I've managed to sneak a look at the house from time to time," said Cal. "There hasn't been any sign of the Carroways or your sister, either. No one has left the house or appeared at a window."

"This isn't good," said Garcia, as he stabbed the ground with his pickaxe, venting a little of his frustration.

Cal noticed Hogue was watching them from a distance.

"The big man's keeping an eye on us," he warned.

He bent over his task, alert for any change. When he paused to stretch, he glanced up at the overlook. No doubt Hendrick was there taking this all in. The kid had been right about one thing: being close to Tate's killers wasn't easy. It had taken all his restraint to stay in control and hide his feelings. He recalled the argument between the cook and Hogue. It didn't sound like Wren was one of the outlaws. Maybe he could be recruited.

"Garcia, were you told anything about the cook?"

His partner paused to wipe sweat from his face. "Very little," he said. "The man who brought the message believed he could be trusted. Wren was the only one. All of the other loyal hands had been fired and run off."

Unaccustomed to hard manual labor, Cal's hands were blistering. They'd put in hours of hard work by the time the triangle signaled mealtime. He and Garcia dropped their shovels and headed for the mess hall. When they got there, the outlaws had already gathered. Cal found a vacant seat at the far end of a long table. Garcia slipped in beside him.

This sure is a friendly place, Cal thought sarcastically when he looked across the table to find Green glaring at him. Ledoux and Coble were giving him the cold shoulder, no doubt remembering that he'd witnessed their humiliation at Dollarhide's. Ledoux's friend, Marsh, was too far down the same side of the table to be easily seen. They were ignored by the others, who seemed to have their minds on food.

Besides Garcia, Wren, and himself, Cal counted nine at the table. Since there were nine outlaws, this meant that no one was on guard duty at the house. He wondered if the prisoners were left unguarded at other times as well.

Having rung the summoning triangle, Wren was keeping them waiting. This didn't sit well with Hogue.

"Hurry up!" he shouted. "You got us here. Now bring on the food."

The cook came hurrying in, grumbling with each step. He carried a large, steaming bowl, which he placed on the serving table at one end. Then he scurried back for the rest. When he was done, the table was heaped with steaks, biscuits, mashed potatoes, beans, and peach pies. The biggest man of all, the one who fit Barley's description, made sure that he was the first in line. Cal and Garcia took their places at the end. There was no question about them being lowest in the pecking order. Cal noticed something odd, though. The foreman, Jared, hadn't been in the lead like you'd expect. He'd followed behind Barley. Could that mean that Barley was edging him out in other ways too?

After sampling Wren's cooking, Cal had to admit that he was good at his job. This was likely the reason Wren hadn't been fired along with the others who were loyal to the Carroways. The one bad thing about the meal was his having to eat it in the company of Tate's killers. Somehow, he had to keep up the act. He also needed to find a way to have a private word with Wren.

After Barley had cleaned his plate twice, he wiped his mouth on his sleeve and looked around the room.

"I think you've all wasted enough time feeding your faces," he said. "There's daylight left and I want you to get back to work. Except for you, Green. You're to take some grub over to the house. We've got to keep the prisoners fed. And Green, keep your hands off of them women. You hear me?"

Cal saw Garcia's facial muscles tighten. Green was the last person who should be given such a task. He noticed that Barley had come right out and called the prisoners what they were. He'd dropped all pretense. Jared gave him a poisonous look but kept his mouth shut. The fact that Barley was giving the orders didn't bode well for the foreman. Cal wondered if this conflict could be exploited somehow. He walked beside Garcia as they went back to work. All the while, Garcia was watching the house.

Chapter Seven

Green was taking his time obeying Barley's order to take food to the prisoners. Cal kept watch on Garcia, who was keeping watch on the house. They were getting very little work done,

Which was all right with him. His muscles were already aching from the unaccustomed labor.

"Your sister will be fine," he said, hoping to reassure his partner, who looked ready to take on the whole gang by himself.

"Green is a dead man if he dares to touch Lucinda. He has no sense of decency at all."

Recalling what the Southerners had told him of Green's actions, and from what he'd seen for himself, Cal figured that sooner or later the young outlaw was going to end up with a bullet between the eyes.

"He's a cold-blooded killer, *mi* amigo. But we can't show our hand yet. Not if we can keep from it."

Green and Carlisle, the outlaw who rarely spoke, were the last of Tate's killers to be named.

"He was supposed to take them food," said Garcia after a time. "Why hasn't he done it?"

"Most likely he's being contrary because Barley gave him an order."

"Or maybe he is waiting until dark, when he thinks no one is paying attention and he can do as he pleases."

It was then Cal spotted Green heading toward the house with a tray in his hand.

"There he goes," he warned.

They tried to look busy while they stole glances at the outline. When Green reached the door he kicked it open and went inside. Seconds ticked away. Minutes passed. Garcia dropped his shovel and stood poised for action. He reminded Cal of a mountain cat ready to spring.

"Steady, friend," he said when he saw Garcia's hand drop toward the borrowed pistol at his side. "Unless the women are in immediate danger, we wait. We don't want to mess up our chance to get them out of here alive."

Garcia took a deep breath and withdrew his hand.

Cal checked his pocket watch. Ten minutes had passed since Green had entered the house. *How long does it take to deliver a tray of food and leave?* He knew Garcia was thinking the same thing.

Before he could replace the watch, the door flew open and the young outlaw stumbled into the yard. He was off-balance and struggling to keep from falling. Women's voices shouted at him in both Spanish and English. Garcia dropped the shovel and started toward the house. Cal grabbed his arm and pulled him back.

"It's over, amigo," he said. "The women took care of him. At least for now."

Green lost the struggle for balance and fell on his backside. He shouted curses as he got to his feet. Then he stomped off toward the barn, his hands clenched into fists. About halfway there, he paused to give the house a backward, venomous glance.

"I think I'm going to have to kill that piece of trash," said Garcia.

"No doubt. But not today, my friend. Not today."

When the sun was behind the mountain, they stowed their shovels and pickaxes in a shed. Then they headed for the barn to retrieve their gear. They were almost there when Barley appeared from around the corner of a building and called for them to stop.

"Just where do you two think you're going?" he said, planting his bulk firmly in front of them.

"We were going to pick up our gear that's stowed in the barn," said Cal, painfully aware that he was inches away from one of Tate's killers.

"And then what?"

Barley seemed to enjoy throwing his weight around, letting everyone know that he was the boss.

"Then we were heading for the bunkhouse. Any objections to that?"

Barley scowled at them. "Yeah, I've got objections. Plenty of 'em. I don't know you or your friend here from my Aunt Tillie's third husband. You're not going to be sacking out in any bunkhouse with me and my men. You can leave your gear in the barn and stay there yourselves."

"Fine with me," said Cal, keeping a hold on his temper as he started to make his way around the human roadblock.

"Both of you remember that I'm keeping an eye on you. So don't try to pull anything."

"Like what?" said Cal.

"Like anything. I've got no patience for saddle bums." Having said his piece, Barley turned and stalked off.

"Amigo, I don't think that fellow trusts us," said Garcia. "In fact, I think he might be a little worried."

And well he should be. If only they'd been admitted to the bunkhouse, they could have gotten the drop on the outlaws while they slept, thought Cal.

"Whether or not he's worried, he sure likes to throw his weight around," said Cal. "I think Jared is starting to find that out."

"So it appears. Barley was only a day ahead of us, yet he seems to have taken over."

"Maybe this split can be encouraged and used to our advantage."

They bedded down in the barn loft without incident, except for Garcia tripping over a cat that worked in the barn as a mouser.

A few hours after dropping off to sleep, Cal was instantly awake. *What had he heard that had disturbed his rest?*

Someone was moving about the loft. Through squinted eyes, he could make out Garcia's form.

"What in blazes are you doing?" Cal demanded to know.

"I need to speak to my sister. She may not have recognized me, and this would be my best chance to get to the house and let her know that I'm here."

"They're sure to have a guard posted."

"I'll watch out for him.

Cal understood his partner's need to see that his sister was unharmed and to reassure her with his presence. Still, he wanted to go to the house. He needed to talk to the Carroways.

"We can't both go," he said, "and I need to talk to the rancher. I'd have gone earlier if I hadn't fallen asleep. Maybe Carroway can help us figure a way out of this. If you want, I'll take a message to your sister."

Garcia reluctantly agreed.

"What am I to do while you're gone?" he said. "I feel so useless."

"Stay by the barn and keep alert. If I'm caught, you're going to have to get out of here fast. Ride up to the overlook and send Hendrick for help."

"Very well. You can depend on me."

Cal slid the door open a crack and slipped through it. For a moment he paused to look around. The light had been snuffed in the bunkhouse and all was quiet there. No guard was in sight. He made his way stealthily across a wide-open space between the barn and the mess hall. Above him, a sickle moon did little to brighten the nighttime landscape. For this, he was thankful.

When he rounded a corner of the building he saw the dark outline of a man. He was sitting on the ground, leaning against one of the outbuildings. Cal moved closer. The man was sound asleep, snoring like a bear. The smell of whiskey tainted the air around him. Cal could just make out the empty whiskey bottle that lay beside him. He recognized the man as one of Coble's outfit, the one called Marsh. For sure, Marsh wouldn't be causing him any trouble. At least not tonight.

He moved on quickly to the main house and went to the far side, out of view of anyone at the bunkhouse. He tapped on a window softly. There was no response. He tapped again, louder.

Within seconds, a shutter flew open and the curtain was drawn back.

"Is that you, Mr. Wren?" someone whispered.

"No," said Cal. "But I'm a friend, just the same. There's another friend at the barn, Emilio Garcia."

"Lucinda," the woman called softly, "this man says your brother is here at the ranch."

Another woman joined her at the window. Both were only voices attached to dark shadows. He caught the scent of lavender.

"Where is Emilio?" she whispered. "Is he safe?"

"Yes, for the time being. He's waiting for me at the barn, but he's worried about you. Jared hired us this morning, but none of them trust us. We're going to try to get you out of here."

"Thank heaven you've come," said the first woman, "but this is going to be difficult. I'm Elizabeth Carroway, and my Uncle Dudley isn't at all well. This takeover has been a terrible blow to him."

"Can he ride?"

She hesitated. "I suppose he can. But not far and not fast. It would be too much for his heart, I'm afraid."

This wasn't what Cal wanted to hear. No doubt it was the rancher's weakness that had tempted his foreman to try a takeover.

"Just be ready for anything," he said. "We'll do what we can. It may be that you'll have to ride out on a moment's notice, and ride fast. I have a friend stationed up on the mountain by that overlook. If anything happens to us, try to get away from here and get up there to him. He'll help you."

"Gracias," said Lucinda. "Please tell my brother that I am proud of him. And tell him to be careful."

He felt them watching as he backed away into the darkness. On his way to the barn, he saw, to his relief, that the bunkhouse was still dark and quiet.

When he reached the door, Garcia was waiting.

"Did you see them?" he asked eagerly. "Did you see Lucinda?"

"Yes," Cal assured him, "the women are fine. I can't say the same for the old man, though. His niece told me he has a bad heart. He can't ride far. Lucinda said she was proud of you and to be careful."

"Perhaps we'd better go inside," said Garcia, nervously glancing about.

Cal followed him into the barn. "Look, I don't think we've got a whole lot of time left. It's plain that Barley doesn't like our being here. On top of that, Jared may be having second thoughts about hiring us."

"I sense this too, but I'm confused. Barley acts like he's the boss, but Jared hired him and he's paying him. Which one is in charge around here?"

"That's a good question. It seems that Barley's not wasting any time. It looks like he's forcing Jared out and taking over the entire operation. If Jared still has any real power, he won't have it for long."

"Then if I were in his place, I'd be getting worried."

"I don't doubt but that he is," said Cal. "It's like that old story goes. When you ride on the back of a tiger, you're likely to end up as its dinner. It looks to me like

Pete Jared picked the wrong tiger to ride when he picked Barley and his gang."

"Then what do we do now?"

"I've got work to do in the morning, so I'm going to try to get some sleep."

Again, he bedded down. Weary from the late hour and his day of labor, sleep wasn't long in coming. It wasn't yet dawn when he awoke with a start and slipped away to have a talk with Wren. He could see lamp light in the cook's quarters and could hear Wren stirring around, banging pots and pans. When he stepped inside, the cook stopped what he was doing and glared at the intruder.

"You're not supposed to be in here," he said. "I'm busy."

"My name is Thornton and I was told that you're loyal to the Carroways."

Wren pulled himself to his full height, such as it was. "What would the likes of you know or care about loyalty?" he said.

Cal lowered his voice. "I'm here to rescue Lucinda Garcia and the Carroways."

The cook's demeanor changed in an eye-blink. "Thank all the Saints," he said. "I've been worried sick about them. What with that weasel Jared out to steal the place and use it for an outlaw hideout, and the others he brought in, there's no telling what they'll do. But who sent you?"

"Nobody. Fact is, I've got my own score to settle with Barley and his outfit. They killed and robbed a couple of good men. One of 'em was the best friend I ever had. I was on their trail and it led me here. This other business was something I didn't expect."

"Who's that fellow with you?"

"Garcia is Lucinda's brother. He got word from one of the former hands that his sister and the Carroways were in trouble."

"Well, at least there are three of us," he said. "Still, there's little we can do for them the way things are."

"You can keep your eyes and ears open. That's what Garcia and I will be doing. We'll look for a weakness that we can exploit or a chance to escape outright."

"Keeping an eye on things is what I do best," he said. "You and your friend watch your step. These are bad men we're dealing with."

Wren went to the door and took a quick look outside to make sure that no one was listening. Satisfied, he closed it and turned back to Cal.

"Thornton, there's something you need to know. Mr. Carrroway's son, Jim, is a doctor in Santa Fe. He's half owner of this ranch, and he'll inherit the other half when his father passes on. He's young and he has connections to the Territorial Legislature. Young Jim is in a position to cause this bunch a whole lot of grief. I hate to say it, but I think Jared's gone and ordered someone to kill him."

So, Dr. Carroway was the mystery man that Barley was supposed to find in Santa Fe. But why hadn't he succeeded? If a prominent citizen had been recently murdered, Señorita Martinez would surely have mentioned it, thought Cal.

"I was told that Barley had been ordered to Santa Fe to find a particular man," said Cal. "It appears that, for some reason, he wasn't able to do that."

"Well, they'll try again, no doubt. There's too much at stake. They've got to get young Jim out of the way."

Cal heard a door slam in the direction of the bunk-house.

"Uh-oh, sounds like they're getting up," said Wren. "It's best they don't see you here."

"I'm leaving," said Cal, who was already halfway to the door.

"I'm glad that you and Garcia are here."

Cal managed to make his way back to the barn without being seen. Later they joined the others for the morning meal. After they ate, Barley confronted them before they could leave the hall.

"You two have some carpentry work to do," he said. "There's boards piled behind the barn. Haul 'em over and build the covers for those two outhouses you dug the holes for yesterday."

To Cal, working with lumber sounded a lot easier than digging. He found the sawn boards where they were stacked behind the barn. No doubt there was a sawmill somewhere in the vicinity.

"Have you done this kind of work before?" asked Garcia, as he positioned a board across a pair of saw-horses.

"Not so you'd notice," Cal admitted. "But how hard can it be?"

"Since I'm accustomed to building with adobe, I'd best watch you for a while, before I begin."

Thanks a lot, he thought.

He shoved his hat to the back of his head and looked the situation over. "I guess we cut some boards the same length and nail 'em together," he said. "Anyhow, since we're going to be watched, we'd better act like we know what we're doing."

Garcia muttered something in Spanish as Cal hefted a saw. It could have been a prayer, or it could have been something quite different.

They hadn't been working long before the outlaw on guard duty shouted, "Hey, somebody's coming!"

Cal looked up to see a lone rider heading their way. He was coming from the direction of the mountains. At first glance, he feared it was Hendrick. However, this man had no spare mount or mules with him. What's more, he was riding an extraordinary horse. It was a beautiful palomino. A sudden thought occurred to him. If Barley had missed the younger Carroway because he was gone for some reason, he might have left a message that would bring the heir back to the ranch. Cal would be willing to bet his last peso that the approaching rider was Jim Carroway, and if he was, he was riding straight into a trap.

Chapter Eight

It didn't take the outlaws long to spot the stranger. Barley, Jared, Green, and Hogue mounted up and rode out a short distance to wait for him. The rest of the outlaws stayed behind. There was nothing Cal could do but watch.

"Could that be Carroway's son?" said Garcia, his work forgotten.

"Most likely. Barley probably left word in Santa Fe for him to come home."

The man reined up in front of the outlaws. Cal could see he was in his late twenties or early thirties. He was clean shaven and neatly dressed. His face expressed intelligence and, to his credit, no fear. He glanced over the rough-looking outlaws until his gaze rested on Jared, who appeared to be a cut above the rest. He seemed to recognize the foreman.

"Pete, I'm sure you remember me," he said. "I'm Jim Carroway. It's been awhile since I was here, but I got your message that my father wanted to see me right away."

Jared must have felt like he'd struck gold.

"One of my men left the message at your office," said Jared. "He was told that you were out of town. I'm sorry to say that your father is ill and I think your place is at his side."

Carroway was clearly disturbed by the news.

"My father is ill? Then why wasn't I told of this sooner?"

Barley and Jared exchanged glances.

"Mr. Carroway didn't want to trouble you," said Jared. "He thought his health would improve."

Jim Carroway was out of patience. "Get out of my way!" he ordered. "I'm going to see what's wrong."

Before he could move, Barley drew the big hog leg he carried and aimed it at the doctor's forehead.

"Just stay right where you are, Doc," he ordered, "and keep your hands where I can see them."

"Pete, just who are these men?" he demanded. "What's going on here?"

"Take it easy," said Jared.

Green rode up and made a big show of disarming the prisoner, which was exactly what he'd become.

"Jared, I demand to know what this is all about," said Carroway. "I'm half owner of this ranch, and these scoundrels have no right to be here."

A good try, thought Cal, but bluster wasn't going to work.

"You don't own nothing," said Barley. "Your father sold his ranch to Jared."

"Oh, I doubt that," said Carroway. "Besides, he couldn't sell all of it. He doesn't have the right to sell my half."

"Which is why you've been sent for," said Jared. "You're going to sign your half of the ranch over to me as well."

Carroway looked at the foreman like he was something he'd gotten on the bottom of his boot in the barn lot.

"I'd die before I'd sign anything over to you," he said. "My father trusted you and you betrayed him. You're nothing but a thief."

Barley laughed, but it was a mean sound without humor. "I guess the doc needs a little persuading before he pencils in his name." He gestured to Hogue, who walked over and yanked Carroway from the saddle. Green bound his hands.

"Throw him into one of the sheds," Jared ordered. "Let him cool his heels for a while. He needs time to think about what's going to happen to him and his old man if he doesn't do what we tell him."

"Maybe you ought to let me work him over first," said Green, his cruel little eyes bright with anticipation.

"Later," said Barley. "Give him a chance to come around first."

"After which, you'll kill me," said Carroway.

"Maybe I will," said Barley. "And then again, maybe not. Anyway, I don't see that you've got much choice."

"What have you done with my father?"

"He's over at the house. Probably got his nose at the window right now, lookin' to see what's happening to you. Them two women are in there with him. Troublesome creatures they are too."

Cal felt helpless as he watched them drag Carroway

to one of the sheds and shove him inside. The door slammed shut and a thick bar dropped into place. Barley was quick to take possession of the palomino.

"He's stubborn," said Jared. "It's not going to be easy to make him turn over the ranch."

"You leave him to me and my boys," said Barley. "He'll be begging to sign that paper before we're through. But I'm not in any hurry. Let him sweat it out for awhile."

"You're going to have to kill him afterward. You can't let him walk away with what he knows."

"I don't have any intention of letting him walk away," said Barley. "You hired me, now let me do my job."

He looked over and saw Cal and Garcia then.

"You two get back to work!" he ordered. "You ain't getting paid to stand around gawking."

It took all of the self-restraint Cal could muster to keep his mouth shut and his hand away from his gun. Before he headed back to the sawhorses, he noticed Jared's expression. It was obvious that the foreman didn't like the way Barley had taken over and was giving orders. Still, he hadn't risked challenging him. No doubt about it, there was trouble among thieves.

Cal busied himself with sawing and hammering. All the while, he thought about the power struggle between the two men. Barley was in control of the outlaws, including Coble and his men. Jared, on the other hand, had no one. The way it looked, his position was every bit as precarious as that of the Carroways. What's more, it was likely he was smart enough to be aware of this.

"Is there nothing we can do to help the doctor?" Garcia wondered aloud.

"Not now, I'm afraid. We're going to have to bide our time and wait for our chance."

"There are so few of us," he lamented. "I'm sure they intend to kill all of the Carroways, and my sister too. With what they know, the outlaws can't afford to let them live."

He was right. But they still had time. They had as much time as Doc Carroway could hold off signing that paper. They were lucky that Barley wasn't in a hurry. Maybe he wanted to get rid of Jared first.

"They can't afford to let us live, either," he said. "They don't trust us and they're not going to take any chances."

"So we wait and watch?"

"For now. If we act too soon, we'll only make matters worse."

They worked throughout the afternoon to finish constructing the two small outhouses. Both turned out better than Cal had expected. They'd just finished when Wren called everyone to supper.

Cal noticed that the cook was curter with the outlaws than usual throughout the meal. No doubt he'd watched the doctor being dragged away and locked in the shed. Barley didn't seem to notice any difference. He acted like he was in particularly good spirits. It was a mood that wasn't shared by Jared.

When Cal finished eating, he didn't linger. Neither did Garcia. They got up and left the mess hall together, but they hadn't gotten more than a dozen steps before Barley called out for them to stop. He'd followed them.

"Uh-oh," said Garcia under his breath. "I do not like this."

"You want to see us?" said Cal.

"Yeah," said the outlaw, catching up to them. "I've got a job for you, Thornton. You're to ride north in the morning with McGill. I want a tally of all the cattle up that way. What's more, I want it to be accurate."

Cal nodded. "I'll see that it is."

"Do you not want me to go as well, señor?" said Garcia.

"If I'd wanted you to go, I'd have told you," said Barley.

Cal was tempted to ask the outlaw when he'd become foreman, but decided not to rile him. *At least not yet.*

"I'll be ready to ride at daylight," he said.

"See that you are," said Barley. Satisfied with his order, he crammed his freshly lit cigar back in his mouth and headed for the bunkhouse.

"Are you thinking what I'm thinking?" said Garcia as they made their way to the barn for the night.

"I am if you're thinking that McGill doesn't mean for me to come back."

"They're planning to get rid of us one at a time. We're too few and they're suspicious, even of Wren."

This was true. Cal knew, sure as sin, he was going to be fighting for his life come daylight. McGill was to be his assassin.

"I'm worried about Lucinda," said Garcia when they reached the barn. "If I get killed and you do not, amigo, I want you to promise you'll come back for her."

"You're not going to get killed. But I promise I'll come back for her."

"*Gracias*. That is all I ask."

During the night Cal slept fitfully. When he opened his eyes, he felt like he'd spent those hours wrestling mountain lions. It wasn't yet daylight when he made his way over to the cook shack to let Wren know about his orders.

"You be careful," said the cook. "I'm sure you're savvy enough to know that Barley doesn't mean for you to come back."

"That's the way I've got it sized up too. I'd be obliged if you'd do what you can to help Garcia and the women."

"I will, but that won't be much, I'm afraid. They watch me like a hawk. Anyway, I wish you luck, my friend."

He held out his hand and Cal grasped it.

"I'd better get out of here before they notice," he said. "No doubt McGill will be coming around soon."

At breakfast, Garcia found a seat beside him. While they ate, they exchanged no words in the presence of the others. He noticed that the outlaws kept sneaking looks at him as if they knew what was in store.

As soon as he finished he went and picked up his gear. Then he headed for the corral to get Coronado. The big horse was at the far side when Cal whistled him over to the gate. Coronado trotted up to him and nuzzled his hand. But before Cal could release him, Barley came striding over.

"Not that one," he said. "Leave him be. You're going to ride that mouse-colored gelding over there. The grulla."

The grulla wasn't anywhere near the horse that Coronado was, and Barley knew it. The outlaw stood there with an ugly smirk on his face, like he was daring Cal to challenge his order. This wasn't the time or place to make a stand. Cal managed to keep a bland expression and do as he was told.

In the meantime, McGill was saddling his own mount. When they were ready to ride, Wren came hurrying out with food packages for their saddlebags.

"Thanks," said Cal, meeting the cook's gaze, which contained a mute warning.

Beyond the cluster of buildings, he and McGill turned northward. The man beside him was a wiry knot of rancor, an assassin with an assignment to kill.

They hadn't gone more than a mile or so before Cal noticed the outlaw was deliberately lagging behind. He reined up and half-turned, waiting for McGill to draw even. He wasn't going to let himself be an easy target for a bullet in the back. When McGill caught up, not a word was spoken. The outlaw's first tactic had failed. No doubt there would be another. Nonetheless, Cal had gotten a message across. He wasn't going to be an easy mark.

On the north range he saw that there was cattle aplenty, as many as the range could comfortably support. He noticed that there was a lot of young stuff that needed to be rounded up and branded, but with Jared having run off all of Carroway's real working hands, most of the work had been left undone.

The high mountain valley got more rain than the west side of the slope, and grass was good here. He figured that the ranch on its own was worth a whole lot. As an outlaw hideout, it was worth considerably more. Cal pulled the tally book from his vest pocket and began his count. Through it all, he never lost track of McGill. He didn't know when the next attempt on his life would happen. He only knew that it would. When it did, he intended to kill the first of Tate's murderers.

The sun was overhead when he took a break to eat. He dismounted and tethered the grulla. McGill watched and mimicked him. The outlaw sat facing him about a dozen yards away. Cal took care to eat with his left hand, a precaution that didn't go unnoticed.

The morning had started out cool, but the sun was warming the valley nicely. A breeze blew the scent of pine from the mountainside. Under other circumstances he'd have found the work on the north range pleasant. But now he was facing a killer who intended to keep him from living out the day.

When they'd finished eating, McGill got to his feet and issued an order.

"Thornton, I want you to ride over and scour that mountainside for stray cows. There's bound to be some up there. Count them and herd them back down to the valley."

Cal tensed. *So this is it.* In order to cover the distance, he'd have to turn his back on McGill. When he did, he wouldn't stand a chance. *Better here and now, and face to face,* he decided.

"Well, Thornton?" McGill taunted. "Don't just sit there like a dumb donkey. Do what you're told."

The knife he carried at his back was suddenly heavy. It would do its work silently if he could only reach it.

"Are you plannin' on killing me, McGill?" he said, stretching his arms neck-high as if to relieve the tension. In doing so, he'd made himself vulnerable. His revolver was an impossible distance away and he clearly had no chance of beating McGill to the draw. Triumph gleamed in the eyes of his would-be killer.

"You don't seem too worried," said McGill as his hand inched toward his sidearm.

Cal casually clasped his hands behind his neck.

"I'm not worried. At least not so long as I'm facing you. You've got the look of a back-shooter."

McGill's features twisted in rage at the insult.

"You're a dead man, Thornton. I've got my orders. If you'd rather see it coming, I can surely oblige."

He went for his gun, believing that his opponent was helpless.

With one smooth motion, Cal drew the knife from the sheath at his back and slung it at the outlaw. McGill's pistol had barely cleared leather before the blade penetrated his heart. He died instantly and toppled from the saddle.

Cal got down and walked over to him. He felt no regret as he retrieved his knife, wiping the blade on McGill's shirt before returning it to its sheath. He picked up the outlaw's gun and packed it in one of his saddlebags. After loading McGill's body on the back of his horse, he mounted his own and rode to a nearby gully. He got down and kicked loose dirt from the side, creating a cavity. When it was large enough, he shoved the body inside and caved enough dirt over the opening to hide it.

"Well, Tate," he said aloud, "this is the first of your killers. He sure won't be troubling anybody else."

The confrontation with McGill had taken only minutes from start to finish, yet it had seemed much longer.

Now that the tension was draining away, he felt tired beyond measure. He also felt a deep sense of relief that he was still alive. Still, the danger wasn't over. There were six people back at the ranch who needed his help. He mounted the gray and gathered the reins of the outlaw's horse. Then he rode off without looking back.

Chapter Nine

Cal headed back toward the ranch. Before he got within sight of it, he stopped to wait for nightfall. Only under the cover of darkness would he have a chance of slipping in and freeing the prisoners. He considered riding to the overlook and sending Hendrick for help, but any help that the kid would be able muster would come too late. He was on his own.

Since the doctor hadn't mentioned seeing Hendrick, he must have hidden himself and the animals when he heard someone coming down the trail.

Cal leaned back against his blanket roll. He needed to rest and gather his strength for what was to come. He noticed a red-tailed hawk circling overhead, searching for prey. It was much like the one he'd see days earlier. A short distance from where he lay motionless, a chipmunk scurried into the brush. Alerted by the hawk's shadow, it had run for its life. The bird of prey would have to look elsewhere for its dinner. *People are like that,* he thought. There were those like Jared and Barley who were always hunting for prey, and victims who'd been unable to scurry to safety like the chipmunk had done.

Time passed slowly as he waited. When, at last, it was dark, he mounted the grulla and took up the reins of McGill's gelding. Then he rode toward the ranch with only the lights in the sky for illumination.

It was well outside the perimeter of the buildings that he dismounted and tethered the horses. Then he quickly exchanged his boots for moccasins. What he had to do this night called for stealth.

All seemed quiet. He headed for the barn, hoping to find Garcia bedded down there. Careful not to make any noise, he slid the door open.

"Garcia," he called softly.

In the moonlight that spilled through a high window, a large figure was suddenly silhouetted. Hogue stepped forward.

"So, McGill failed to kill you, did he? Well, I'll see if I can't do better than him."

The outlaw was bringing his gun to bear. Cal grabbed for his own, knowing that he didn't stand a chance. Hogue was thumbing back the hammer when he toppled sideways with a grunt. Cal didn't waste any time. He dove for the pistol. The outlaw knocked him back, forcing him to let go. While Cal struggled to his feet, Hogue grabbed a handful of his hair, using it to twist his head until his neck was exposed. One blow would crush his wind pipe. Cal kicked out, wondering why Garcia didn't come to his aid. His moccasin-clad foot did little damage. Hogue was bringing up the gun. Marshaling all of his strength, Cal struggled to wrench his way free, but he could only get one arm loose. He reached back and drew the blade from its sheath. The angle was awkward, but he managed to plunge the knife into Hogue's big gut. The outlaw gasped and dropped his gun.

"You've killed me," he said, surprised that such a thing could happen.

"It needed doing," said Cal. He picked up Hogue's gun before returning his blade to its sheath.

Muffled noises emanated from the shadows. He went to investigate. It was Garcia. His hands were tied to the support post and he'd been gagged so he couldn't shout a warning. It was Garcia who'd saved his life by kicking Hogue off balance. He cut his partner loose.

"Is he dead?" Garcia asked as soon as the gag was removed.

Cal took another look. "Yep. He's dead as he's ever going to be."

"What about McGill? What happened on the north range?"

"He bought it too. He was going to shoot me down, thinking I didn't have a chance. I had a weapon he didn't reckon with."

"That knife?"

"Yes. It's a handy thing to have."

"So it seems. You and McGill were scarcely out of sight when Barley got the drop on me. They brought me here and tied me up. Hogue was my guard. It appears that Barley didn't entirely trust McGill to get the job done. If McGill failed to kill you, he figured you'd come back for the others, and that you'd come here first."

"Are the others safe?"

"Yes, so far as I know. I think Hogue would have said something if any of the prisoners had been killed."

"What did they do with your gun?"

"They took it. I can't seem to hang on to one anymore."

"Then when you get the circulation rubbed back into your hands, I suggest you take Hogue's. I've got mine and McGill's."

Garcia bent down and picked up the .44. He checked to make sure it was loaded before sticking it in his belt.

"What now?" he asked.

"We'll alert Wren and have him get the horses ready. Then we'll move on and free the doctor from that shed. That'll make three of us to get the old man and the women out of here."

They moved like wraiths across the open space between the barn and the cook shack. The bunkhouse was dark now. So was the house. There was no sign of a sentry.

Cal's gentle rap on the cook shack window was answered immediately. Wren looked relieved to see him.

"We need your help," he said, when Wren opened the door.

"I'm glad you made it back, Thornton, and that you're all right too, Garcia. Come on in. Quickly, *now*."

They stepped inside the dark interior.

"I need you to go over and saddle enough horses for the prisoners and yourself. Make sure to get that big gelding of mine while you're at it. The one called Coronado."

"I'll do it. What happened to Hogue?"

"He's out of it. So is McGill."

"Good news. But you be careful, 'cause Barley is jumpy as a spooked doe. A new man rode in today that Barley don't trust. Fellow claims he's a friend of some of Coble's kin. He calls himself Barn Oak Phipps."

Cal was surprised to hear the name. Somehow, Barn Oak had broken out of his cell at the Santa Fe jail and come straight to the Carroway ranch. It was like he knew right where to go. It must have been that Coble passed along the information to his kinsman, who in turn told Phipps. Cal figured it was a good thing he wasn't around when Phipps rode in.

"We'll try to free the doctor now," he said. "Then we'll go to the house. Be ready."

"Count on it," said Wren.

Leaving the cook to his task, they made their way over to the shed where the younger Carroway was imprisoned. Garcia got the job of lookout while Cal lifted the heavy bar. Laying it aside, he opened the door and looked in. It was black as a coal mine. While he wasn't able to see anything, he could smell the presence of a man and hear him breathing. He took a step inside.

"Dr. Carroway," he called softly. "We're friends and we've come to get you and your family away from here."

Carroway must have been asleep, for he gave a start.

"Who are you? Is this some kind of trick to get me to sign?"

"I told you, we're friends. Garcia here is Lucinda's brother."

"The woman who helps my sister?"

Cal was growing impatient. "Yes. Now, come on while there's still time."

This got Carroway to moving. He left his makeshift

prison behind and breathed deeply of the crisp night air.

"Whoever you are, thank you," he said. "I won't be much help though, for I don't have a gun."

Cal handed him the one he'd confiscated from McGill. "Now you do," he said. "I trust you know how to use it."

"I grew up on a ranch. Of course I know how."

"Then wait here with Garcia. I'm going after the prisoners. If there's trouble . . . Well, Garcia knows what to do."

"I think we should go with you," said Garcia.

"No. One will have a better chance of slipping past the outlaws than three. You two are backup in case something happens."

He left them and went toward the house, keeping to the darkest places. Once he paused to listen. All was quiet at the bunkhouse. Again he went to the far side of the house. The shutters were closed. He tapped softly and waited. A minute hadn't passed before he heard someone moving around inside. Soon the shutters were unlatched and one of them was opened a crack.

"Who's out there?" It was Lucinda Garcia's voice.

"The friend who spoke to you earlier. The doctor is already free. He's with your brother. I've come to get you away from here. Tell the others to hurry."

"Elizabeth is with me, but Señor, the outlaws came and took Mr. Carroway this morning. I do not know where."

Cal felt like he'd been hit. This was something he hadn't expected.

"You and Miss Carroway had better come with me," he said.

"Wait. I will only be a moment."

He could hear the women moving around in the darkness. True to her word, it was only a moment before Lucinda Garcia was back. She opened the shutters wide and he could tell she was clad in riding clothes and a jacket.

"They have secured the doors," she said, "but not the windows."

With his help, she climbed over the sill. Elizabeth Carroway was next. So far the plan was working. Now if they could only get to the horses before the alarm went up.

The three of them made their way quietly past the bunkhouse. There was only a short distance now to the shed where Garcia and Carroway were waiting. He trusted that Wren had brought the horses to them by this time. Just a little farther and they'd have a chance. They were almost there when someone shouted. Then a shotgun was discharged.

"Run for the shed!" he yelled at the women. "Keep your heads down."

He stayed behind to hold off the outlaws and give the others a chance. A light went on inside the bunkhouse. Men were pouring out the door, shouting and cursing as they came. Cal kept low, so as not to make himself an easy target. The outlaws began firing into the darkness at random.

He prayed that Wren had the horses ready to go, and he hoped that the others didn't wait around for him. As the outlaws rushed forward, he fired into them, trying to slow them down and give them something to worry about.

During a lull, he heard the sound of horses making their getaway. Good. Now, he had to keep the outlaws busy for as long as he could. There wouldn't be time to reload. He wished he'd kept the gun he'd given Carroway. That had been a mistake. He figured he had two shots left. He started to fire when something slammed into him. The gun dropped from his hand and the ground came up and hit him. He turned his head so he could look up at the sky. *Strange,* he thought, *the stars are winking out.*

Chapter Ten

Pete Jared couldn't say exactly what it was that woke him from a fitful sleep. He lay there in the dark, listening. Wind thumped against the outer walls of the bunkhouse and whistled around the corners. Inside, snores came from the neighboring bunks. There appeared to be nothing to cause alarm.

He raised himself on one elbow. Barley was sleeping nearby, covered by a mound of bedding. Though arrogant and dangerous when awake, he was now as helpless as a newborn babe. How he hated the man. The temptation to reach for his gun and put an end to his troubles was almost more than Jared could resist. Only a healthy sense of self-preservation held him back. Green was sleeping one bed away. The trigger-happy young outlaw was a little bit crazy, and he was loyal to his boss. Beyond Green was Ledoux. He was Coble's man. Still, it was likely he'd back Barley too. Marsh, another of Coble's men, had been given guard duty. He was more than likely holed up somewhere asleep, for there was no one to guard against. He'd made it clear he resented the assignment, especially since Hogue was out in the barn keeping watch.

A feeling of desperation washed over him, and he was close to despair. His plan had been so perfect, yet he'd gotten himself into a mess with no way out. At least none that he could think of. How could he have let a two-bit outlaw like Barley take over and humiliate him the way he'd done? The truth was he'd misjudged him. He hadn't suspected the intensity of Barley's ruthlessness and greed. Neither had he considered the fact that Barley's men would be loyal to their boss, while Jared had no allies. He knew, by now, the way the outlaw boss thought, and had no doubt that Barley had marked him for death. His only hope was to kill Barley first, and that would be a daunting task. He didn't trust anyone, and he was rarely alone.

Jared sighed softly and eased himself back. Carlisle, Coble, and that new fellow, Phipps, had taken old man Carroway from his home. There'd been no reason for that except intimidation. A hard ride and camping out in the elements would only aggravate his illness. But a lot Barley cared. He figured the separation would put pressure on both father and son to sign the papers giving the ranch over to Barley. After they'd done it, he'd have to kill them. He'd kill the women too. Old man Carroway was anything but dumb. He'd have had that figured right off. There was no way he was going to sign.

Had he managed to stay in charge, things would have gone smoothly. He would have been subtle, except for insisting on marriage to Elizabeth. As a nephew, he'd have run things the way he wanted, and his claim to power and profits would have been legitimate. The ranch was paying well on its own. Establishing a hideout for hunted outlaws would have made him rich beyond his wildest dreams. But his plan had gone up in smoke, and he lived in constant fear.

He heard the noise again and wondered if McGill had returned. This time Barley heard it too, and wasted no time scrambling out of bed and pulling his boots on. In the moonlight Jared watched him grab his shotgun. But before he could get to the door, Marsh yelled.

Barley stepped outside and shot into the darkness. The others scrambled to join him.

Jared took care to hang back. He'd been guilty of many things, but shooting at Elizabeth wasn't going to be one of them, and likely she was out there.

The others were yelling and firing now. He hoped that Elizabeth had gotten away. Barley and his gang were too busy to notice that he wasn't taking part in the battle.

All of a sudden the noise stopped. The quiet was eerie. Barley sent Green and Marsh forward while he waited.

"Hey, we got one of 'em!" yelled Green.

"Which one?" said Barley, hurrying up to have a look for himself.

"It's Thornton, the one McGill was supposed to take up to the north range and kill."

"Well, it appears that McGill wasn't man enough to do it. I should have known. He's probably dead and it serves him right."

"What about Hogue?" said Green.

"Marsh, go have a look in the barn. He's probably

dead too. If he ain't, I intend to kill him. He was supposed to take care of Thornton if he came back, and then get rid of that Mex friend of his."

"I think Thornton's alive," said Green. "Can I finish him off?"

"Just a minute," said Jared, stepping to the front. "Maybe he can tell us where the others headed, and who else knows about our little operation. It's a fact that somebody had to send him. He didn't just happen to ride up here on his own."

Barley turned that over in his mind.

"You're right," he said at last. "Jared, you and Green take him to the bunkhouse and see what you can do for him. I'll be there to question him when he's able to talk."

Marsh came running up then. "Hogue's dead. I guess Thornton killed him and cut Garcia loose. Wren's gone too."

"That's about what I expected," said Barley. "I've got a bunch of donkeys working for me."

Jared got Thornton to the bunkhouse with some help from Green. Barley followed close behind. A lamp had already been lit. They eased the wounded man onto a bunk. He was still breathing but he was out cold. A smear of blood marked the place where a bullet had grazed his skull. Jared took a wet rag and washed the blood away. Had the bullet hit a fraction to the right, Thornton would be stone-cold dead.

One thing for sure, he wasn't an ordinary saddle bum. It would take a skilled, savvy man to get the best of McGill and Hogue both. Jared figured him for a lawman. Somehow old man Carroway must have gotten the word out. If he was right and Thornton was a lawman, others would know where he was—and why. Jared's possibilities were limited and unappealing. Unless he could figure out a third alternative, and get very lucky, he was either going to die from a bullet or face a long term in the Territorial prison.

"Watch him," Barley ordered. "When he comes to, I want to know it. First he talks. Then I get rid of him. Tie his hands good and tight so he can't cause trouble."

When the others had left, Jared went over and stood looking down at him. Thornton gave a low moan and his eyelids fluttered open. When he caught sight of Jared there was recognition in his eyes. He grabbed for a gun that wasn't there. Jared signaled him to be silent.

Keeping an eye on the prisoner, he backed over to the door, opened it, and stepped out to look around. Assured that Barley hadn't left anyone behind to spy on him, he went back inside.

Thornton looked puzzled but said nothing. Jared dragged a stool over beside the bunk and sat down.

"We're in the same boat," he said. "I was thinking that maybe we can help each other."

Thornton looked suspicious, but he mouthed the word "how."

Jared got up and fished a half-empty bottle of whiskey from among his things and poured a little into an old coffee cup. Then he lifted the prisoner's head and put the cup to his mouth, enabling him to take a few sips. The whiskey seemed to help.

"I don't know how you got the best of McGill," he said, "or Hogue, for that matter. But any man who can take care of those two isn't some ordinary down-at-the heels saddle bum. Barley's figured that out too. He intends to kill you as soon as he finds out who sent you. In other words, he needs to know who he's up against, as well as how much they know. He'll also want to learn where the Carroways and your friend Garcia are headed. He'll be tracking them come daylight, but he likes to know what he's getting into."

"You realize that Barley's going to kill you too," said Thornton. "He wants it all for himself."

Jared nodded. "I know. I made a big mistake hiring him and his outlaws."

"You've made yourself an outlaw too. You started all this."

The accusation hurt him, even though it was true.

"If I could undo what's been done, I would. None of this was supposed to happen. I didn't think Barley or anyone else could simply ride in and take over like that."

Thornton struggled to sit up and managed on the second try. "What did you mean about us helping each other?" he said, shaking his head to clear his vision and wincing at the pain it caused.

"I'm not sure how, but I'll do what I can for you. I want you to do the same for me. I'll start by cleaning that wound."

Jared found some alcohol and a bandage among the supplies that his former boss had made sure to keep on hand. Then he cleaned the area the bullet had grazed and wrapped the bandage around Thornton's head.

"When they come back, stall as long as you can," he warned. "Pretend you're still unconscious. It'll hold back the rough stuff for awhile. When they do start questioning you, don't tell them what they want to know, for as soon as you do, it's all over."

"I need my gun and I need to get out of here. So do you."

Jared hesitated. Their chances of success were slight. But there was no chance at all for either of them if they stayed.

"We need horses, and they won't let us near the corral," he said, eyeing the closed door.

"I've got two saddled horses waiting close by," said Thornton. "All we need to do is slip out of here without them spotting us."

It sounded like it might work. "Let's do it," he said.

Jared went to his bunk and retrieved Thornton's gun where he'd stashed it underneath. He pulled a rifle from its place on the back wall and handed both to Thornton, who was now on his feet. Jared had his own rifle, along with his sidearm, and plenty of ammunition for both.

"If we snuff the lamp, they'll be sure to notice," he said. "I'll go first and look around. If the coast is clear, I'll give a low whistle."

There was a light at the cook shack. Since Wren had taken flight with the others, Jared figured they were feeding their faces as best they could in preparation for what was to come. He gave the signal and Thornton appeared beside him.

"This way," said Jared's new ally.

They made their way through the darkness, always listening for a sign that their absence had been discovered. The horses were waiting in deep cover a short distance beyond the ranch buildings. Thornton took the precaution of leading them farther away before mounting and riding off.

He'd done his part by arranging the escape from the bunkhouse. Now it was up to Thornton to get them away. Once he was free of the Barley gang, he'd worry about freeing himself from the law, which he was certain Thornton represented. Why else would he have come to this remote valley at precisely the time the Carroway ranch was being seized?

Moonlight was scant but they could see well enough to ride. They made a wide circle of the ranch. Once they were on the west side, they headed directly toward the mountains. By the time the sun was getting ready to appear, they were climbing into the Sangre de Cristo Mountains. Their luck had held. Barley and his men wouldn't pursue them in the dark, but now it was coming on daylight.

"I'm curious as to where we're going," Jared said at last.

"To meet friends" was his cryptic answer.

It wasn't long before that meeting took place. Gathered near an overlook were Garcia and his sister, Wren, Elizabeth, Jim Carroway, and a kid that Jared hadn't seen before.

"Thank heaven," said Lucinda when they rode up, though she gave Jared a look of scorn.

He didn't mind that so much, but it pained him the way Elizabeth turned away from him. Jim Carroway wasn't happy to see him, either.

"You're hurt," said the kid, eyeing the bandage on Thornton's head. "Are you all right?"

"I'll live. I got the same kind of scratch you got back in Kansas, Hendrick. I can sympathize with you a little better now."

"Well, I know for a fact that you've got to be hurting like the dickens."

Thornton shrugged and turned to Garcia, who wanted his attention.

"What is he doing here?" Garcia demanded to know, indicating Jared. "In case you've forgotten, he's the enemy."

Jared kept his expression free of emotion. He'd been prepared for this kind of reception.

"After I was shot, they took me prisoner," said Thornton. "Jared dressed my wound and helped me to escape."

"You mean he's changed sides?" said Lucinda

"It looks that way."

He felt a surge of annoyance. They were talking about him as if he couldn't hear them.

"I'm on my own side," he said. "It was prudent for me to leave. Thornton was my ticket out."

"Barley was going to kill us both," said Thornton. "Right about now, they'll be tracking us. We've got to get out of here."

"But what about Uncle Dudley?" said Elizabeth.

"I don't know where he is," said Thornton, "but Jared might have some idea."

They were all looking at him now.

"All I know is they headed south, along the base of the mountains. They can't go far because Mr. Carroway isn't well enough to travel a great distance. I do recall an old abandoned cabin down that way. It's on the mountainside. I mentioned it to Barley once. It's among the trees and can't be spotted from the valley. It's a good hiding place and I suspect that's where they took him."

Elizabeth looked relieved to hear that Barley was concerned about keeping her uncle alive, at least for a time.

"What are we going to do, now, amigo?" said Garcia, addressing Thornton. "We await your orders."

Jared noticed how easily Thornton wore the mantle of leadership.

"Hendrick and Carroway, you'll wipe out our tracks," he said. "Let's not make it too easy for them. We'll move deeper into the forest. There we can hide and get some food and rest. In a few hours you, Jared, and Carroway will go with me to find and rescue the old man. Wren and Hendrick, you're to stay with the women. Hide them and see that they're protected.

"I want to go with you," said Hendrick. "I've waited up here all this time by myself. Now I want to take part."

Thornton gave the kid a hard look. "This is against my better judgment, but you can go. Remember, though, the rule about following orders still applies."

"Right. I won't forget. Thanks."

They all moved deeper into the forest before they stopped to rest. Wren passed around pieces of cold corn bread and bits of dried beef that he'd managed to take from the cook shack before his escape. Thornton was wolfing down his share like he was half-starved. Truth of it was, Jared was hungry too. It didn't taste bad, but he hoped that this wasn't to be his last meal on Earth.

He didn't look forward to a showdown with Barley, Green, and the others. Still, it was better to meet them face to face, armed with a .44, than to be shot down like a dog. If it was in the cards that he was going to die, he intended to die like a man.

Chapter Eleven

Matt Barley stood in the doorway of the empty bunkhouse. He was mad enough to strangle somebody with his bare hands, and he didn't much care who it was. None of this was going the way he'd planned. First of all, McGill hadn't been able to follow one simple order. Then Hogue went and got himself knifed and let Garcia escape. Even worse, the prisoners got away. Now Jared was gone, taking Thornton with him. There was Wren too, but that gnome of a cook didn't count for much anyway.

This had been a good setup that he'd happened into, one that would have made him rich beyond reckoning. But because of the dummies who worked for him, the whole thing was turning sour. Still, it wasn't over. Not yet. He had another ace up his sleeve.

"The sun is coming up," said Green. "Are we going to track 'em down now?"

It didn't surprise him that Green was eager to be on the hunt.

"No," he said. "I've got a good idea about where they'll want to go, and Jared is just the man to lead them there. When they arrive, we'll be there waiting."

"Yeah, that's right," said Green. "They'll be going to free that old man."

His expression reminded Barley of an old hound dog that had just treed a coon.

"How do you know we can get there ahead of them?" said Marsh, who'd been listening. "They've got a sizeable head start."

"Because I heard them ride due west for the mountains. I ordered Coble and the others to take Carroway south along the edge of the foothills. There's an abandoned shack hidden in the trees. That's where they're holding him."

"If we can get there first and add our firepower to that of the other three, we can wipe 'em out the first time they make a move toward the cabin," said Green. "Looks like things are going our way after all."

No thanks to the likes of you, thought Barley. "Let's get a move on," he ordered.

When he got to the corral, Barley saw that Wren and the prisoners had taken his best horses. At least they hadn't taken all of them, or run them off. He picked out a black gelding with white stockings and threw a saddle over its back. The gelding would have to do. The others groused a little about the mounts that had been left, but by the time Barley had the cinch tightened, they were all ready to ride.

"They might be watching us from somewhere up on the mountain," said Ledoux. "There are places up there where you can see the ranch clearly."

Barley was aware of that, but he doubted they'd hang around to spy on the ranch when they had old man Carroway to see about.

The four of them headed south. Then they turned and made their way to the base of the foothills, before continuing on in the same direction. Jared had reminded Barley about the cabin, but it was already known to him. Years ago, before he'd gone back east, he'd hidden out there once. Whoever had built it was long gone.

In the silence of the ride Barley thought of his days with Captain Quantrill. He was a king back then. They were all kings. They'd held up supply wagons, and they'd stolen payrolls. They'd ride into towns, terrorizing the civilians and taking everything of value. They'd kill the men and some that were almost men, and put the fear of God into everyone else. Then they'd leave the buildings in flames. He'd never forget Lawrence or Baxter Springs. Those were the days. But it all ended in Kentucky when Quantrill was wounded near Louisville and later died. He figured it had started to end before that, when the bushwhackers were forced to split up. He'd been lucky to get out alive, though he'd never managed to hang onto any of the loot he'd stolen. It was like it had been cursed. The bushwhackers had been the scourge of three states, but all he had left when the war was over was a taste for violence and a hatred of Kansans. It had been a pleasure to kill those two sodbusters on his way to New Mexico Territory. It had been mildly profitable, as well. Now, those horses that he'd taken had been stolen away from him, in turn, but he intended to get them back.

"Do you think Coble and Carlisle can hold their own

if Thornton and his outfit get there before we do?"
Ledoux asked, interrupting his thoughts.

"They ought to, even if they're taken by surprise.
They have that friend of Coble's cousin with 'em. That
Barn Oak fellow."

"Do you trust him?"

"Not one bit further than I trust you."

The jab silenced Ledoux. But it was the truth. He'd
learned long ago that he couldn't trust anybody. There
wasn't a man in the world who wouldn't betray you if
the price was right. And there were some who'd sell you
to the hangman for a drink of rot gut.

"How far away is this place?" said Green, impatient
for action. That was one of the things Barley liked about
him. When it came to a fight, he was never a slacker.

"Not far," he replied. "I didn't think the old man could
stand a long ride."

They'd taken to the mountainside when he spotted
the cabin. It was barely visible, hidden as it was among
the pines. Barley signaled them to stop and called out to
Coble. When he got a response, they rode in.

The three men had been playing cards. The remains
of their breakfast lay on a table in one corner. The old
man was lying on a pallet at the other end of the room,
close to the fireplace where a fire had been laid.

"Have any trouble?" Barley asked, glancing around
the cabin.

"No," said Carlisle. "The old man don't look too good,
though. We fixed him a bed and fed him some soup. He
didn't give us any trouble."

To Barley's eyes, Carroway looked even weaker than
before. Maybe that would make him easier to deal with.

That is, if he didn't decide to die. But right now, there were more urgent matters to worry about. Thornton and his rescue party were apt to show up any time now. Thornton would, no doubt, be in the lead. There would also be Garcia, Carroway's son, Wren, and that turncoat Jared to back him up. Maybe they'd arm the women too. Thornton didn't look like the type to hide behind women's skirts, but that Lucinda Garcia was strong-minded and full of sass, and some of it had rubbed off on Carroway's niece. It was possible the seven of them could soon be facing as many as six guns. They had the advantage of surprise, though, for the enemy would be expecting only three guards. They also had the thick-walled cabin, and while it wasn't exactly a fortress, it would afford them protection from the attackers.

Green stepped outside to look around. He was jumpy as a frog on a hot griddle. Barley couldn't blame him. He was feeling that way himself. It was like he'd thrown the dice and was waiting to see how they'd land. One thing for sure, he'd bet everything on this single cast. Those dice had better land right.

Over in the corner, the old man had a coughing fit. Barley didn't like the sound of it.

"Throw another blanket over him," he ordered. "He looks cold."

It was Barn Oak Phipps who grabbed a blanket and followed his order. He wondered about the bearlike out-law. He'd been one of Coble's cousin's men, but that didn't recommend him as far as Barley was concerned. He'd met Shorty Coble once, and sized him up as strictly small time. He'd never do anything that involved a lot of risk. What's more, he doubted if Barn Oak Phipps had transferred his loyalty. That is, if he ever had any to transfer. On the other hand, he doubted if any of them felt loyal to him. He couldn't inspire it, not the way Captain Quantrill had done.

"Marsh, go put a pot of coffee on," he ordered. "It may be that we're going to have to wait a while for the party to start."

"Do you think Thornton will be able find this place?" said Coble, as Marsh hurried to do as he was told.

"I know that Jared can find it. And when he does, it's going to give me a whole lot of pleasure to get rid of him."

"But you were planning on killing him anyway," said Carlisle.

"True. But I'm going to enjoy it a lot more now."

The minutes ticked by. They were all restless. Waiting was hard. It always had been. Given a choice, he'd rather be in the thick of battle than standing around waiting for one to start.

The old man stirred.

"Is he worse," said Green, "or is he just pretending?"

Barley went over and looked down at him. He'd lost weight and there was a sickly color to his skin.

"If he's pretending, he's doing a right fine job of it," he said.

He went out on the rickety front porch and looked up the steep slope. They'd launch their attack from above. There were too few of them for a pincer movement, so they'd be all together. Most likely they'd ride down whooping and shooting like avenging angels. They were going to be in for the surprise of their lives.

Chapter Twelve

Cal felt better having gotten some sleep and food. He glanced around at the others; two women, the men he trusted, and one man that he didn't trust at all. He noticed that Hendrick was awake too, and was watching him.

"You got something on your mind?" said Cal softly.

"I was just wondering if you plan to wait until dark to storm that cabin."

Cal got up, pulled his gun from its holster, and checked it before giving an answer.

"The way I see it, trying to make our way through this mountain forest at night without a trail to follow wouldn't be wise. Besides, riding down and storming that cabin is a surefire way to get the old man killed."

The kid looked confused. "Then what do you have in mind to do?"

Cal gazed into the distance as if looking for an answer in the clouds.

"I'm going to find the cabin and look the situation

over," he said at last. "The rest of you will stay hidden close by until I need you."

"And what do you want Mr. Wren, Elizabeth, and me to do?" said Lucinda Garcia, who'd been listening. "Are we supposed to sit here in the middle of the forest and worry about whether you're dead or alive?"

"Mr. Wren will escort you both to Taos."

"And what would I be doing in Taos? I can shoot. I can make a difference. So can Elizabeth and Mr. Wren. It seems to me that you need all the help you can muster."

"That's true," said Elizabeth, getting to her feet. "Uncle Dudley's life is at stake. I'm not leaving."

Cal choked back what he wanted to say. It wouldn't have been fit for their ears. The truth was, he had no idea how to deal with women, especially two hardheaded women like Lucinda Garcia and Elizabeth Carroway. They were trying to stare him down and they were succeeding.

"All right," he relented. "If you insist on going with us, you and Elizabeth will have to keep well back from the cabin. You're to stay with Wren and follow orders. If anything happens to us, you have to get away and ride to Taos. Tell the law what's been going on here."

"Agreed," said Elizabeth. "We can do that."

The sun was a couple of hours past its zenith and they could ill afford to linger. It was possible, even likely, that Barley would anticipate their move and go straight to the cabin with his men.

"Get ready to ride," he ordered. "Jared, you know where this cabin is located, so you take the lead."

When they were mounted, Jared led them single file through the thick-needled pines. The branches slapped at them, scratching exposed skin on hands and faces. The going was slow.

The sun angled farther and farther to the west as they rode southward. It didn't seem to Cal that they were making any progress at all. Then, suddenly, Jared reined up and signaled for them to stop.

"I'm sure the cabin is close by," he said. "It'd be farther down the slope, though. It wasn't far from the valley floor."

Cal listened, trying to hear any sound that would betray the outlaws. There was nothing but the whisperings and chirpings of nature that one would expect. It grated at him that the cook and the women had come along. He had a bad feeling about it. They'd come in spite of his objections, so now they'd have to take their chances.

"Stay here," he told the others, "and keep hidden. There's still enough time for me to ride down to where I can see the cabin, have a look, and get back."

"What if they're all there waiting for us?" said Hendrick.

"Three of them are, for sure," said Jared. "And Barley and the rest of them will be on their way if they're not there already. You can bet on it."

"Be careful," said Lucinda softly.

Without wasting any more time, Cal headed down the steep slope. Coronado was sure-footed, but at one place the big gelding lost his purchase and slid downward a ways on the slick pine needles. While he struggled to regain his footing, branches smacked Cal's face. He tasted blood. After that, the going was better. It wasn't long before he spotted smoke rising from a chimney. He kept under cover and moved in closer.

When he'd gone as far as he dared on horseback, he stopped and tied Coronado's reins to a low-hanging branch. The rest of the way he went on foot. When he came to a young pine that offered just enough cover, he stopped. The makeshift corral was filled with horses. Barley and the others had arrived. Cal had scarcely taken his place before Green stepped out the door. The young outlaw leaned against the wall of the cabin to build a smoke. There were seven of them now, and the cabin was a veritable fortress. Plus they had a sick old man held hostage.

While he watched, Carlisle came out and spoke to Green. Whatever he said caused the young outlaw to laugh. Cal was tempted to move closer, but he didn't dare. It was too risky.

A frontal assault was apt to get him and all who'd joined him killed. Yet a frontal assault was clearly what the enemy expected. In this case, stealth was needed, along with a showy diversion.

All the while he'd been reconnoitering, Cal avoided looking directly at Green or Carlisle. It was during the war that he'd learned how a man could sense when he was being observed. An enemy could also spot the slightest movement. He waited, motionless, until both outlaws had gone back inside. Then quietly he made his way to Coronado. Together they went to join the others who were waiting for him on the mountainside.

"What happened to you?" said Hendrick, gawking at his welted, bleeding face.

"I ran into a little difficulty, is all," he said, for there was no time to waste explaining the trivial.

"Gather round," he ordered. "This is what we're going to do."

With an economy of words he outlined his plan.

"Do you think it will work?" said Elizabeth, unable to hide her doubt and anxiety.

Cal had to admit that she was a beautiful woman, but he had a higher regard for Garcia's sister. Lucinda had some starch in her backbone.

"It would have the best chance of succeeding," assured her cousin. "Besides, Liz, anything we try will entail risk. There's no getting around it. That's why it's important for you and Lucinda to stay back here, far from the cabin, and be ready to ride."

"I understand," she said, though Cal wasn't sure she did.

"When are you going back down there, Mr. Thornton?" Lucinda inquired, for that was the plan.

He glanced at the sky. "Soon. Garcia, Hendrick, Carroway, and Jared, you're to wait until the sun is about to set over the mountains. Then create your diversion. Make a lot of noise. Get their attention. But stay back so they don't get a clear shot at you. If they come after you, get out of there fast.

"Why wait?" said Hendrick.

"You'll be coming down the slope from the west so they'll be looking into the sun. That just might make all the difference. I'll ride down first and be in place near the cabin waiting for you to start the ball. While they're busy with you, I'll grab Mr. Carroway and get him out of there."

"There's a back window," said Jared, "in case you weren't where you could spot it. It's your best chance."

He was glad to have that piece of information; still, the only reason he trusted Jared was because the foreman was acting in his own best interest. They had a common enemy. For now, they were allies.

While they watched, Cal started on his return journey, only this time he took a roundabout route. For one thing, he didn't want to risk Coronado losing his footing again. He also wanted to approach from the back side of the cabin, since the outlaws' attention would be out front. When his allies started their diversion, he needed to be close to that back window and ready to act. There wouldn't be a minute to lose.

He didn't much like this plan. It was way too simple and predictable. Too much could go wrong. But it was the only one he could come up with, and that sick old man was running out of time.

When he reached a place where he could see the back wall of the cabin through a canopy of green, he dismounted. He tied Coronado's reins before sneaking in closer. The window was right where Jared said it would be. Luck was with him. The shutters were open.

He looked up and saw that the sun had slid closer to the crest of the mountain range. Garcia and the others would be on the move. As he stood there motionless, he fancied he could feel his heart beating. A buzz of voices drifted outward from inside the cabin. He couldn't quite make out what they were saying. Step by careful step, he moved in next to the wall.

Someone was cooking beans and onions. The smell was unmistakable. To his dismay, his stomach growled loud enough that he could hear it. He rammed a fist against the complaining organ and willed it to be quiet.

He could hear the voices clearly now. One that had a French accent demanded to know if the beans were done. It was the Frenchman, Ledoux.

From the sound of it, Marsh was a lot more concerned about an attack.

"Are you sure they'll come here?" he said. "It seems to me they'd want to save their own hides. Old man Carroway ain't nothin' to Thornton. He ain't nothin' to that Garcia fellow, either."

"Are you so dumb that you think those two just happened by?" said Barley. "Somebody sent Thornton and Garcia to do a job. I wouldn't be surprised if Thornton's a Pink."

"One of the Pinkertons?" said Ledoux, to whom this was a new and unsettling thought.

"Aw, them Pinks ain't nothin'," said Green. "They die when they're shot same as everybody else."

"I can tell you for a fact that Thornton handles himself real well," said Phipps. "He's not carrying that sidearm just for looks. Strange thing, though. Up in the mountains he was partnered up with a redheaded kid."

"Garcia sure ain't no snot-nosed redhead," said Marsh. "You sure we're talking about the same man?"

"No doubt the kid took off on his own," said Phipps. "He was hardheaded and dumb as a stump. Garcia must be somebody he happened on to."

"Or a partner that he met up with," said Barley. "They might even be deputy Federal Marshals. Leastwise Thornton might be, and you can bet that Garcia is working for him, whatever he is."

The sun sank lower. *Come on,* Cal urged his allies silently. *What's holding you up?*

"Dish up them beans," Barley ordered. "I'm hungry."

Suddenly, a shot broke the silence. It came from somewhere above, on the mountain.

"What the . . . ," said Barley, running for the door and slamming it open.

More gunshots followed. The rest of the outlaws gathered at the door and front window.

They laid down a barrage of gunfire that caused the attackers to withdraw and ride away. Then they raced to their horses and set out after them.

The plan was working. Cal swung his leg over the sill of the window and dropped inside. He stumbled and narrowly missed stepping on the elder Carroway, who was lying on a pallet.

"We've got to get you out of here, Mr. Carroway," he whispered. "Are you able to ride?"

The old man stared past him with a stricken look. Something was wrong.

"Well, Thornton, this is a real pleasure." The familiar voice came from the shadows in the far corner of the room. Cal spun around to find himself looking down the business end of a Walker Colt. Barn Oak Phipps was holding it. When the commotion started, he'd stayed behind.

"It may be a pleasure for you," said Cal, "but not for me. How'd you get out of the Santa Fe jail?"

"Let's say I've got an understanding of human nature, plus that sheriff underestimated me. Now, empty your holster and put that gun of yours on the table. Careful now, I got an itchy trigger finger."

Cal did as he was told. He figured he had little time before the rest of the outlaws returned. Another volley of gunshots was heard in the distance. He hoped that his friends had gotten away.

"Idiots!" said Phipps. "Barley and the rest of 'em are too dumb to figure the gunplay was a diversion so you could get in here and steal the old man away."

"Can't everybody be smart like you, Barn Oak," said Cal, who was desperately trying to think of a way out. "Now, why don't you let me go? There's no point in holding me."

It was a feeble attempt, but he had to try. Phipps laughed.

"It seems to me there's every reason to hold you. First off, I've got a score to settle. I only wish that red-headed brat was here with you."

From the corner of his eye, Cal saw the old man sink back on his pallet, the picture of hopelessness. As he stood still as a statue, he wondered how long Phipps would be able to keep the heavy revolver pointed at him. The question was soon answered when the outlaw pulled out a stool and sat down at the table. There he propped the heavy gun, taking care to keep Cal in his sights.

"Now, we just make ourselves comfortable until our friends get back," he taunted. "They'll be right glad to see you."

Try as he might to figure a way out, Cal was stumped. There was nothing he could do but wait. The old man was no help at all. In fact, his eyes were closed as if to block the unpleasant situation from his sight and mind.

When Phipps heard the sound of returning horses, he

grinned, displaying a mouthful of tobacco-stained, rotted teeth.

"Guess the party is about to start."

Barley was first inside the cabin. He jerked to a halt when he saw Cal standing there in front of the Walker Colt.

"They drew you out of the cabin with gunplay so Thornton here could snatch the old man," said Phipps.

"That why you stayed behind?" said Barley, glaring at him. "Guess you're so smart you had it all figured out."

If Phipps had wanted to be admired or rewarded for the capture, he was to be disappointed. In fact, Barley appeared to resent him. It was plain that Green didn't like being made a fool of, either. He looked on the verge of exploding with rage.

"Coble, tie this badge-toter up," Barley ordered. "And Phipps, you can take that grin off your face and put that hog leg away before you shoot somebody."

"Yeah," said Green. "You might shoot yourself in the foot."

Phipps gave him a withering look, but did as he was told.

When Cal's hands were bound, Barley approached. Without warning the big outlaw struck him across the face with the back of his hand. Cal's head jerked back and blood dribbled down his chin.

"Now, I want to know who it is that you work for," he said, his bearded face close to Cal's.

"I work for myself."

"Don't give me that. Are you a Pinkerton or a Federal Marshal?"

"Haven't you got that figured out yet? You're supposed to be a smart fellow."

Barley hit him again. His ears rang from the blow.

"I want straight answers and no more of your smart mouth," said the outlaw. "I want to know who I'm up against."

"I know," said Phipps, from his place by the stove where he was dishing up a bowl of beans.

"Know what?" said Barley.

"I know what Thornton is all about. That redheaded kid let it slip."

Barley turned on him. "Well, out with it!"

"That kid's pa was murdered by five men. They rode up to his Kansas soddy and shot him. Then they took off with his horses. The kid said that Thornton had a friend who was done the same way. Thornton here is out for blood. He's out for revenge, pure and simple. He's after your hide, Barley, and that of the four who rode with you that day. He's already got two of you, though— McGill and Hogue. I guess that leaves you, Carlisle, and Green."

After the treatment Phipps had just received, he seemed to take a measure of satisfaction in needling Barley.

"Is that right, Thornton?" said the outlaw boss, watching his expression.

"I guess if Phipps says so, it's got to be," he replied.

Barley backed off then.

"Guess I'm going to have to take care of you."

"I understood that was your plan to start with. McGill thought so, anyway."

It was a jab that found its mark.

"How did you get away from McGill? He was one of the best."

Cal shrugged. "Guess he got careless this time. I wasn't an old man that he could sneak up on and kill."

The remark earned him a blow in the gut. He doubled over in pain and struggled to keep from throwing up.

"What about them others?" said Green. "We should've stayed on their trail."

"It's gettin' dark," said Barley. "I didn't want to get lost or ambushed up there in the pines. Now, if you want to take off after 'em again, you know where your horse is."

Eager as Green was for the kill, he backed off.

"What are you going to do with this one?" he asked. "Want me to get rid of him?"

Barley looked annoyed. "I'll let you know when I do," he said. "For now, get that lamp lit and bring me a bowl of beans."

Coble approached, took Cal by the shoulders, and shoved him down against the wall.

"Stay put and don't cause trouble," he warned.

They hadn't checked for his knife, but there was no way he could get to it. Even if he could, he wouldn't have a chance against all of them.

As he watched the outlaws eat, his stomach started growling again. It had been a long time since he'd eaten. It looked like it would be even longer before he'd eat again—if ever.

Chapter Thirteen

The outlaws had turned back. Hendrick, Garcia, Carroway, and Jared joined Wren and the women. The diversion they'd staged had been exciting. In fact, it had been the most exciting time of Hendrick's life. He felt like he was doing something useful at last. Something to help bring his father's remaining killers to justice. Hours passed, though, without Thornton's return, and he began to worry. While the others slept, he paced despite the darkness and his own weariness. Even considering Thornton was riding double with old Mr. Carroway, he should have been back. Something had gone wrong. He might even be dead.

"Why don't you try to get some sleep, amigo?" said Garcia from his blankets. "There's nothing that any of us can do tonight."

"I can't sleep. Pa's killers are down at that cabin, and Thornton is likely in trouble."

"If it's any comfort to you, remember that two of your father's killers are dead now. They both tried to kill our friend Thornton, and they both failed. He is a resourceful man and dangerous to his enemies."

"Aren't you worried that they might have killed him?"

"Death is always close by when dealing with men like Barley. But get some sleep. You'll need to be alert in the morning."

Hendrick went over and spread out his blankets, but he was troubled.

"Garcia, I've been wondering about something. Why did Barley and his outfit break off from following us? They didn't stay on our trail very long."

"No. We acted like we wanted to be followed and that finally sunk into Barley's brain. He decided to find out what we were leading him and his men away from."

That meant they may have caught Thornton before he was able to rescue the old man and get away.

"I'm worried," he said.

"We are all worried. For the moment, there's nothing we can do. Go to sleep."

Hendrick crawled beneath his blankets. Exhausted, he slept.

Cal had been in bad spots before, but none worse than now. His bound wrists were raw from trying to work them loose, and he ached from the beating Barley had given him. Five of the outlaws were bedded down in the cabin, while Carlisle and Marsh stood guard outside. Barley wasn't taking any chances. Old man Carroway hadn't moved a muscle and appeared to be half dead. *These lowlifes never give a fellow an even chance. They prey on victims like Carroway and Tate and on women like Elizabeth and Lucinda.*

He leaned back and closed his eyes. If he was going to get out of this alive, it was up to him to figure a way to do it. Fact was, he might not get out of this one. He pushed the thought away.

It was then he sensed a movement in the darkness. The smell of medicinal rub grew stronger and the wheezy breathing of a sick old man drew nearer. He felt cold hard metal being thrust into his bound hands. A knife. Somehow, the prisoner had gotten hold of a knife. Without a word from either, Carroway went silently back to his bed, leaving Cal with a ray of hope.

The knife was sharp. He twisted his wrist and sawed it back and forth across the rawhide strips. It didn't take long for him to cut through and free himself. His gun had been dropped in a corner, several feet away. Trouble was an outlaw was sleeping in front of it. In the darkness, he could barely make out shapes, but the snores were like beacons. He held the knife in case he needed to use it. Step by step, he crept over toward the corner. Holding his breath, he reached across the sleeping outlaw's outstretched legs and felt around for his gun. Seconds seemed like minutes before his fingers touched the grips of the .44. He drew it from the corner and retreated back to his place. Now he had to figure how he was going to get himself and the old man out of there without getting killed. He inched along the wall toward the window. Very little moonlight found its way inside, but there was enough to make out Dudley Carroway. The old man waved his hand for him to go on alone. He had no choice. If he were to escape, he'd have to leave Carroway behind. He nodded his thanks and climbed out the window.

No sooner had he gotten his footing than he spotted Marsh. He could tell because he was taller than Carlisle. The outlaw had his back to the cabin, looking toward the mountain, the direction from which they'd been attacked. If Marsh made a noise and roused the others, all would be lost. After glancing around to see if he could spot Carlisle, he slipped up behind Marsh and brought the butt of his revolver down on the outlaw's head. Marsh didn't even let out a moan as he slipped to the ground.

Now he had to deal with Carlisle. Keeping low, he made his way to the other side. Carlisle was leaning his back against the far end of the ramshackle porch, watching the horses.

There was no way to reach Coronado without dealing with Carlisle first. The idea didn't pain him overmuch, for he hadn't forgotten that Carlisle was one of Tate's murderers. Still, the sleeping outlaws were only the thickness of the cabin wall away. He would have to act swiftly and decisively. He pulled out the knife that old man Carroway had given him and closed the distance in three long strides. Carlisle turned, but before he could shoot or cry out a warning, the knife stilled him forever. The horses smelled blood and started milling around. He had to act fast before one of them whinnied an alarm. It took him a minute to locate Coronado. No one had bothered to unsaddle him. For this Cal was thankful. As soon as he was mounted, he released the other horses from the makeshift corral. They didn't need much encouragement to stampede. They wanted away from the blood smell.

The outlaws heard the retreating horses, and one of them opened the door and peered out.

"What's going on?" he demanded. It was Barley.

Cal urged Coronado forward. The big horse took off in the opposite direction from the stampede. Without horses, the outlaws wouldn't be able to follow him. He hated having to leave Carroway behind, but there was nothing he could do about that, at least not now. He wended his way upward. The going was treacherous in the filtered moonlight. He wasn't certain where his friends were. They may have been forced to move their camp. He only knew they wouldn't ride off without learning what had happened to him. One thing for sure, he was going back to rescue that old man who'd saved his life. What's more, Barley was going to pay.

He doubted the outlaws would go after their horses before daylight, since they were all on foot. Once they'd rounded them up, though, they'd be combing the mountainside. Barley would be hot for revenge because he'd knifed Carlisle and knocked the daylights out of Marsh.

Coronado had taken him a long distance away from the cabin when the last of his strength abandoned him. He got down and tethered the horse. Then he pushed together a bed of pine needles. His head barely touched their fragrant softness before he was fast asleep. It wasn't until he felt the warmth of sunlight on his face that he opened his eyes. Coronado was nearby, munching on a patch of grass. A squirrel scolded him from a nearby limb. *How long past dawn had he slept?* The outlaws would be rounding up their horses by now. That is, if the animals hadn't come back on their own to be fed. One thing was sure, as soon as they had mounts, they'd come looking for him.

Cal got to his feet. He was still sore from the working over Barley had given him. He was hungry too. It had been a long time since he'd eaten an honest to goodness meal. But that would have to wait. The first thing he did was scatter the pine needles he'd slept on and wipe out any other sign that he'd stopped there. Then he mounted up and headed toward where his friends were likely camped. There was no path to follow, and there was the danger of getting lost. Still, he trusted his sense of distance and direction. It was his trail the outlaws would be following now. Barley wanted revenge. So did Barn Oak Phipps. Green just liked to kill.

Barley was furious that the prisoner had escaped from under their noses. He'd been hog-tied and guarded by seven men. Thornton must be some kind of magician to have freed himself and gotten away. Not only that, he'd killed Carlisle without waking anyone, and he'd put a knot on Marsh's head the size of an egg.

"How are we going after him without horses?" said Green, a scowl on his face.

"It don't look like we're going to, does it?" said Barley. "This Thornton fellow ain't near as dumb we took him to be when he hired on. Fact is, he's made fools of all of us."

Mac Coble was coming back up the slope, lantern bobbing with each step. "The horses headed for the valley," he said. "We've got no choice but to go after them on foot come daylight. Catch one and the rest will be easy, I think."

"Once we get mounts, Thornton had better watch out," said Green. "Them others had better watch out too."

"Well, at least we have the old man," said Ledoux. "They're not going to ride off and forget about him."

That was the one bright spot in this mess, as far as Barley was concerned. Thornton hadn't been able to get the old man out. Still, he wasn't about to make his way down to the valley traveling by shank's mare and run around after a bunch of horses. Not while he had men working for him. Let them do the work.

Ledoux, Green, and Coble started down the mountain on foot shortly before sunrise. Each had been allowed nothing more than a cup of coffee to sustain him. Barley had no intention of letting them linger for breakfast. It was a good thing that the cabin wasn't far above the valley.

Marsh was in no shape to go along or else he'd be on his way too. Barn Oak Phipps, on the other hand, was quite capable of hauling his considerable backside downhill, but he was far too lazy. Nothing short of a confrontation would have sent him off, and no doubt he'd have come up with some excuse not to exert himself. Besides, Barley admitted, Phipps' gun would be needed if Thornton or any of his outfit returned to grab Carroway while the others were gone.

He realized he was hungry. "Get busy and cook me some breakfast, Phipps," he ordered. "Then give the old man something to chew on. See that he gets a drink too. I don't want him dying on me yet."

It gave him a measure of satisfaction to see the resentment on Phipps' ugly face. It was clear that he hated to be ordered around. Still, without a word, Phipps obeyed.

After stuffing himself with bacon, biscuits, and dried peaches, there was nothing left for Barley to do but wait. Time passed like a slow-crawling snail. He went to the window a dozen times, hoping for a glimpse of his men returning. On the thirteenth, he was rewarded.

"They're back," he said.

He was waiting on the porch when they rode up. In addition to their own mounts, they'd rounded up the others as well. Coble had four horses on a lead rope—Carlisle's, the one Marsh had been riding, and the two that him and Phipps had thrown saddles over.

"Can we get something to eat now?" said Green.

Much as Barley wanted to say no and get started up the mountain, he was wise enough not to. Green could only be pushed so far.

"Hurry it up," he said. "There's some biscuits left and some bacon. Don't take all day."

"I believe I'll stay behind and guard the old man," said Phipps.

Barley's patience was at an end.

"You're coming along. Marsh can guard the old man."

"Marsh can't even see straight. How's he going to do any good?"

"That ain't your worry now, is it? Get your sorry hide out there and mount up."

If looks could kill, Barley reckoned he'd be dead twice over. But Phipps wasn't running this outfit, and it was time he learned it.

When the others were done feeding their faces, they joined him and Phipps outside.

"Let's get this done," he said.

The sun was high in the sky when the five of them began following Thornton's tracks up the mountainside. Barley did some thinking on what Phipps had told him.

That first old man he'd killed must have been Thornton's friend. They must have been real good friends to bring him all this way and go to all this trouble. He had happened onto that Kansas soddy along with Hogue, McGill, Green, and Carlisle. They'd killed that old sod buster and stolen his horses and mules. Far as Barley was concerned, the old man was asking for it, out there alone like that. Besides, he was Quantrill's man through and through. He hated Kansans.

"He's got a big lead on us," said Ledoux, when they'd been on the trail for a while, "and no doubt he rode over those rocks up yonder. Finding Thornton isn't going to be easy."

Barley didn't expect it would be. But he had to get Thornton. He was a dangerous enemy. Of the five of them who'd raided that Kansas soddy, only two of them were still alive.

Chapter Fourteen

Lucinda had been relieved to see her brother ride up the evening before with the others. They'd been brave to do what they did, taunting the outlaws, making them ride away from their stronghold. Thankfully the gang had broken off the chase. But even that was bad news, for it looked like Thornton may have been caught. That was bad for Mr. Carroway, as well. She felt sorry for Elizabeth. She was in obvious distress. Mr. Carroway's son was more stoical. Either his emotions weren't as strong or he was good at not showing them.

Everyone was awake now, and Mr. Wren was cooking breakfast. There was little to work with, but he'd brought along plenty of coffee.

While they were eating, Elizabeth stood up and addressed them.

"We need to go back to that cabin and rescue my uncle. I'm talking about all of us this time."

"It would be better for us to wait until Thornton returns," said Garcia.

"We all know that he's dead," she said in a matter-of-fact way that caused Hendrick to wince.

"Actually, Liz, we don't know that," said the doctor. "Garcia is right. We need to wait a while longer."

"But your father may be dying," she insisted. "Don't you care?"

It was Carroway's turn to wince. "I care, Liz, but I don't intend to get all of us killed because I'm not thinking straight."

Her face flushed as she stood over him. "So you're accusing me of not thinking straight? Shame on you, James."

Garcia spoke up. "I must agree with the doctor," he said.

"It's only fair that each one of us has a say," said Lucinda, not wanting the situation to escalate. "I think we should take a vote."

"All right," said Elizabeth. "We'll vote."

"Then I say we wait," said Garcia.

"We wait," said Carroway firmly.

"I vote for waiting," said Wren.

"We wait," said Jared.

They all looked at Hendrick.

"I say we wait for Thornton."

"And you, Lucinda, what do you say?" asked Elizabeth, her face drawn.

Feeling almost like a traitor, she answered. "I think we should wait."

"Then I stand alone," said Elizabeth, coldly. "So be it. But if my uncle is found dead, I consider you all to blame."

Lucinda was hurt by her friend's attitude, but she knew she'd done right. She watched as her brother got up and turned away. He went over and retrieved his gear. Then he threw a saddle over his mount.

"What are you doing?" asked Hendrick.

"I'm getting ready to ride. When Thornton comes in, we might not have time to do this."

"Then I'll get ready too."

They all followed suit and Lucinda was glad. It took their minds off Elizabeth's accusation. That they were doing something seemed to ease Elizabeth's mood considerably, as well. They'd scarcely finished when they heard someone coming.

She saw her brother's hand go to his pistol. Then she saw Thornton emerge from the forest, riding that big gelding he called Coronado. A huge sense of relief washed over her.

"You look like the dickens," said his partner, Hendrick. "What took you so long?"

Thornton climbed down off his horse. "I ran into some trouble. Took me a while to get back here."

"My uncle," said Elizabeth, rushing over. "What has happened to him?"

"He's frail but he's still alive. In fact he saved my skin back there. He wanted me to go on alone because we both couldn't get out of there without getting caught."

"Are they on your trail?" asked Garcia, trying to see beyond him.

"Probably are by now, or they will be soon. But I bought some time by running off their mounts. They headed for the valley, and the outlaws will have to go after them on foot and round them up."

"Have you got another brilliant plan?" said Jared sarcastically.

"I don't know how brilliant it is," Thornton replied, "but I do have a plan."

"Well, I expect we'd all like to hear it."

Lucinda noticed that Elizabeth was giving the traitor a look of disgust. Jared was on thin ice as far as she was concerned. Everything bad that had happened to her and her uncle was Jared's fault, and she wasn't about to forget it.

"We're going back to the cabin," said Thornton. "They'll be tracking me, so we'll go down a different way."

"So while they're up here on the mountain, we'll free Mr. Carroway," said her brother. "I like that idea."

"Then shall we get started?" said Elizabeth.

"One moment," said Wren. He pulled an extra pistol and holster from his saddlebag. Then he turned and handed them to Lucinda.

"Careful now, that .44 is loaded," he cautioned.

"Thank you," she said simply and fastened the belt around her waist.

They were all armed except Elizabeth, who didn't seem to mind.

Single file, they began to make their way down the mountain, this time by a different way. Thornton was in the lead. Lucinda and Elizabeth rode between young Hendrick and Mr. Wren. They were well down the slope when they heard the sound of horses and voices some distance away. The outlaws were following the trail that Thornton had made on his escape from the cabin. Thornton gave the signal for quiet. They stopped and waited for the outlaws to put more distance between them, and to get out of earshot. Then they started on again.

* * *

Cal felt a sense of apprehension when the cabin came into sight. He hoped the brave old man was still alive. Before he could dismount at the front porch, Elizabeth was already out of the saddle and calling out her uncle's name.

He was lying on the pallet where Cal had last seen him. He didn't look any better or any worse. Nearby, Marsh lay dead. Somehow Carroway had sneaked away another weapon and had found the strength to stab the injured outlaw. Garcia and Jared dragged the body outside.

"Liz," said the old man. "Is that you? What are you doing here?"

"We've come to take you home, Uncle Dudley," she said, kneeling and kissing him on the forehead. "Are you strong enough to ride with one of us?"

"Pa," said Doc Carroway. "It's me, James."

"Son, I didn't think I was ever going to see you again," he said, his voice trembling with emotion.

The doctor looked him over and felt his pulse. "I think he's a little dehydrated. Bring some water, Liz."

She brought a dipperful to her uncle and helped him to drink. All the while, Lucinda stayed near the door. She could tell that Thornton was anxious for them to get going. He stayed on the porch and kept glancing up the slope.

"Carroway," he said at last, "we'll help you carry your father to your horse. You're to ride with him to the ranch, where you can take care of him. The women, Wren, Hendrick, and Garcia will go with you. You may need to defend the place if things don't go well here."

"What are you talking about?" said Hendrick. "What about you?"

"I'm going to wait here for the outlaws to return. So is Jared. Both of us have a score to settle with Barley."

"Well, it's not as if I don't. I'll stay too."

"No. They're going to need your help at the ranch if Jared and I fail."

"You won't fail," said Lucinda. "I know you won't."

Why she said that, she didn't know. The odds of two against a half dozen men weren't good.

If she'd been calling the shots, they'd all stay together. That way they'd outnumber the enemy. In addition, they'd have the cabin fortress too. But Thornton had his own way of doing things, and she and the others owed him their loyalty.

When they rode out, she glanced back and saw that Thornton was inside. Jared, however, was across from the cabin porch, hidden in a stand of trees. *They can do it,* she told herself. For insurance, she said a quick prayer.

All the way back to the ranch, she strained to hear the sound of gunfire. Once she thought she had, but she could have been imagining it. No doubt she was too far away to hear anything.

Once they got to the ranch, they got Mr. Carroway into his own bed. His son stayed with him, using his medical skills to make him better. Elizabeth hovered close by his side. Lucinda felt the need for air and went outside. Her brother seemed to be in charge now. He was over by the corral, and she went to talk to him.

"Where are the others?" she asked.

"Wren is trying to scrounge enough supplies to fix a meal. Hendrick is doing some out-riding. He's to fire two shots if he sees Barley or any of his outfit heading this way."

"I'm worried about Thornton," she said. "I'm even worried about Jared. He deserves to go to prison, but he's one of the two men who stand between us and those outlaws."

One look at her brother's face told her that he was worried too.

"They should have gotten to the cabin by now," he said. "By tomorrow, we'll know the outcome."

"Tomorrow, we may be fighting for our lives."

He put his arm around her shoulders. "You should have stayed home and gotten married," he said softly. "You might have lived longer."

What he didn't say was that he might have lived longer too. She felt badly for having dragged him into this. Still, she was glad to have him here.

Hendrick ranged farther south. Garcia had ordered him to ride out and watch for the outlaws, but he didn't specify how far he was to go. The old man was in a comfortable bed with his son and his niece beside him. Garcia and Wren were well able to guard the place, and Garcia's sister was as good as any man. Besides, he was only doing what he'd been told to do, he reasoned. By nightfall, he was halfway to the cabin.

He thought of his father and how much he missed him. His murder had been so senseless. Now, three of his killers were dead. Thornton had gotten them all. Maybe now it was his turn.

Alone and in the dark, this thought kept him going. Suddenly, he heard gunfire—a lot of it. He kicked his horse in the sides and set him to a faster pace. No doubt about it, Thornton needed his help.

Chapter Fifteen

Cal watched until Garcia and the others were out of sight. He felt a sense of relief that the old man had been rescued and the women were on their way to a place of relative safety. But the feeling was only momentary. Now came the waiting.

When Barley failed to find them, it wouldn't take him long to figure out what had happened. He'd be back. Then it wouldn't take him long to realize he had them outnumbered. But if he could take Barley out, the others were likely to fold. Except for Green. Green was a little crazy. He'd have to be taken out too. But then, Green was one of Tate's killers.

He glanced through the doorway and spotted Jared half hidden in the new pine growth across the way. No doubt he was sweating it out too.

The outlaws had left Cal's rifle behind, or maybe the old man had managed to hide it. Anyway, he found it in the cabin along with his knife. He'd slipped the knife into its sheath and seen to it that both the rifle and his

.44 were loaded. He had a supply of ammunition, thanks to Wren's foresightedness back at the ranch.

While he waited, his thoughts returned to the war and to the life he'd made for himself afterward. Except for his brief stint as a lawman, he'd been on the go from one town to another. There'd been nothing to keep him tied to any one place, so he'd kept on moving. Mostly he liked the job of buying and selling as he played the part of a trader or peddler, as Hendrick would say. He liked the profits he'd made most of all. Tate would have been a good business partner if he'd had the chance. They'd have had fun traveling around the country together, and it wouldn't have been so lonely on those long rides. But all that was in the past. The truth was, he might not make it through the night. If he did, he was going to start over. Maybe he'd settle down someplace that he could call home. He was starting to envy people like the Carroways and the Garcias. Each was a family where people cared for one another. Family was something he'd always been short on, especially after he'd lost his father. And then he'd left Tate behind to fight for a cause he believed in. A stray thought crossed his mind unbidden. *It doesn't have to stay this way. You don't have to keep wandering.*

He played with the notion for a moment and tried to imagine himself settling down in one place, maybe finding a good woman and raising a family. Then he shook his head to clear it. This wasn't the time to be woolgathering. When the outlaws attacked, there wouldn't be much warning.

The sky was overcast. Rain clouds had formed around the peaks, as he was told they often did. No doubt it would pour later on.

He was sitting just inside, watching through the doorway, when he saw something move across the way. His hand went to his pistol. It was Jared. He raised up out of his hiding place and sprinted for the cabin.

"What's wrong?" said Cal, stepping back as the foreman stumbled across the threshold.

"There's something I have to tell you. Whatever happens, we've got to kill Green. He's had his eye on Elizabeth ever since he got here. She'll never be safe until he's dead."

What he said was true. Cal had seen the way Green looked and acted.

"No doubt he'll be in the thick of things," Cal said. "One of us is sure to take him out. Watch for Barley too. He's the one that's causing all this."

"I know," said Jared. "He's the biggest mistake I ever made."

To Cal's way of thinking, Barley wasn't his biggest mistake. Jared made that when he crossed the line and turned himself into an outlaw. Still, hiring Barley might prove to be fatal.

"You'd better get back to your place," Cal said. "Barley's not a man who's long on patience. I doubt if he'll wander around looking for us much longer. In fact, he's probably found our trail down the mountain by now."

Jared hesitated. "I don't suppose there's anything left around here to eat?"

He reminded Cal of Hendrick, who always had his mind on the next meal.

"The outlaws left a few biscuits and some strips of jerked beef. Help yourself."

After taking a portion of what was left of the food,

Jared went back to his hiding place, leaving Cal to his vigil.

He began to experience an uneasy feeling. It was like the one he had when Barn Oak Phipps and those other two were after him. He could sense that Barley was close.

There was no window facing toward the mountain, so he stayed inside the doorway. By standing on the far side and looking out to the left, he could see the trail that Barley was likely to use. So far, nothing was moving.

The clouds were spreading and would soon blanket the valley. He noticed that the wind had died down. On the surface everything seemed peaceful, but as sure as the storm was going to break, the outlaws were going to attack.

While he was taking a drink from a canteen that had been left behind, his waiting came to an end.

"Thornton!" Barley shouted. "We know you're down there and we're coming to get you."

"Come on then!" he yelled.

He could see them moving closer. It was time. He threw up the rifle and squeezed off a shot. It was instantly answered with a barrage of gunfire. Cal ducked back as bullets pounded the cabin wall. Jared started firing from his hiding place behind a couple of windfall logs.

Then the firing tapered off and became sporadic. There was little that Cal could do now. The cabin was turning into a trap. It was time to get out. The back window faced away from his attackers. Once more, it was his escape route. With his rifle in hand, he climbed through the opening. Staying low, he made his way to deeper cover. He didn't intend to abandon Jared, who was keeping the outlaws at bay, but he'd needed to get out of that cabin.

Using a tree for cover, he fired off a couple of shots in the direction of one of the outlaws. Then he moved quickly. He'd scarcely taken a step before a bullet slammed into the tree where he'd stood.

Suddenly he was under heavy fire. So was Jared. It was time to move out or be killed. He hoped Jared had it sized up the same way.

Ducking low, he ran to the hidden place where he'd picketed Coronado. Wasting no time, he climbed into the saddle and urged the roan deeper into the woods. If he could circle around behind the outlaws, he figured that he and Jared might have a chance.

He was working his way through the brush when the shooting stopped altogether. The sudden silence was downright eerie. *What is Barley up to now?* His view of the cabin was screened by the wilderness.

There was no sound from Jared. He'd made a run for it, or else he was dead. There was nothing to do but continue the fight alone. If he could get behind the outlaws, maybe he could pick them off one by one.

He hadn't yet worked his way around when he saw a flash of light from the corner of his eye.

"What the . . . ?" he said aloud.

As he watched, flames began to consume the cabin. Barley hadn't cared that the fire he'd started would soon spread throughout the forest, destroying all life in its path. He wanted Cal and Jared dead, and he didn't care how he got the job done.

The smell of smoke made Coronado nervous, and the big roan was getting hard to handle. Cal said a prayer of thanks that the wind had died. Had it not, the fire would have spread too swiftly for anything or anyone to escape. As it was, the flames were spreading fast on their own, consuming everything in their path like a hungry dragon. The cloud cover served as a light reflector, turning the sky orange.

Cal's head wound throbbed and he coughed as his lungs filled with smoke. Barley would expect him to make a run for the valley. They'd be waiting to pick him off. Instead, he climbed. His plan was to head north to the overlook once he was well above the flames. From there he'd head for the ranch. Garcia and the others would need all the help they could get once Barley was through playing with fire.

A bolt of lightning startled the horse. It was all Cal could do to stay in the saddle.

"Steady, boy," he said. "It's nothing to worry about."

Before he could get Coronado settled down, thunder rumbled across the mountain. The heavens opened and drenched the mountainside. Peering through a thick curtain of rain, he could see that the fire was being put out. The storm that had been brewing for hours had saved the wilderness.

He wondered about Jared again. In spite of what the foreman had done, Cal hoped that he'd survived. For one thing, the man had saved his life. In a way, he owed him. Then too, his gun was needed.

He paused long enough to drag a waterproof poncho from his bag and slip it on. He was already wet, but it would protect him against the chill and further soaking. Now that the fire was no longer a danger, Cal changed his plan. He'd ride straight down the mountain. They'd need him at the ranch as soon as he could get there. If he ran into Barley, or any of the others, then it was too bad for them. He'd come from Kansas to avenge a murder. This was as good a place as any. Dead, they couldn't harm the women at the ranch, or his friends.

From all around him came the stench of burnt, wet wood. The clouds were moving on and stars were beginning to show.

He'd almost reached the place where the cabin had stood when the figure of a man stepped from the shadows. It was Green.

"Well, well, Thornton, I reckoned you'd be coming back this way," he said. "I've been waiting for you. You see, we've got something to settle."

Green's gun was pointed right at him. He didn't stand a chance.

"Were you afraid that I'm a faster draw than you?"

"I've seen what you did to Carlisle and Hogue. No doubt you killed McGill too. I'm not taking any chances."

"What happened to your friends?"

"I ain't got any friends. Barley and the others are headed for the ranch. They're taking it back."

"But you stayed behind."

"Barley's orders. I'm to find and kill you. You've caused him too much trouble."

Cal still had the knife in his belt that old man Carroway had given him. He inched his left hand under his poncho, while his gun hand stayed in sight. If he could only keep the outlaw talking until he could grasp the weapon . . .

"I never liked you from the first time I set eyes on you," said Green. "Killing you is going to be pure pleasure."

The knife was in Cal's hand now—if he could get it free of the poncho.

"Any last words?" taunted Green.

There wasn't time to free the knife from his poncho and hurl it at the killer. He needed to stall a few seconds longer.

"I guess you've got nothing to say," said Green. "Well, it's time to get down to business then."

"Wait!" Cal shouted.

At the same time, a shot rang out. Green's expression was one of disbelief as his hand touched a blossoming stain on his shirt. He dropped the gun and fell.

Cal dismounted and went over to make sure the outlaw was dead. Then he glanced around for the shooter.

"Over here," said Jared, stepping from behind the burned skeleton of a pine tree.

"Thanks," said Cal. "I'm glad they didn't kill you."

"Not more than I."

He came up and nudged Green's body with his toe. "I guess he won't be bothering Elizabeth any more, or her friend, either."

It was plain that he wouldn't.

"Now I guess we'd better get back to the ranch."

"You can bet Barley's on his way right now. Have you got a horse?"

"Do you see a horse?"

"Only the one I'm riding."

"Then I expect we ride double. Let's get a move on."

Jared climbed up on Coronado's back and they set off toward the north. The outlaws had a lead. Still, it wasn't much of one.

Chapter Sixteen

Barley's mood was as foul as the weather. Rain poured off his hat and he shivered in the cold. He'd lost another man that he badly needed. On top of that, Thornton and Jared had gotten away. He hoped Green found and killed them.

"I sure wish I had some dry clothes and a hot meal," said Phipps, breaking into his thoughts. "I expected that bunch would be easy to deal with. It's Thornton who's giving us all the trouble."

"Yeah," said Coble, "from what I've seen that hombre must have nine lives, just like a cat."

Barley ignored them both. The clouds were moving off, taking the rain with them. It was his bad luck that the fire had failed to smoke Thornton and Jared out of hiding. The threatening storm had broken too soon.

"Are we going to attack the ranch tonight?" said Coble. "Or do we wait?"

"No waiting. We'll attack as soon as we get there. Maybe we can take 'em by surprise."

"What happens then?"

"Then we get rid of some of our problems."

Hendrick heard the outlaws coming toward him and backed off to the side. He'd been paralleling a shallow arroyo, and now he used it as a cover. They passed by, maybe thirty yards away, headed for the ranch. Garcia and the others had to be warned. Thornton would simply have to wait.

The sudden downpour had quenched the forest fire. He was glad of that. He'd seen prairie fires sweep across miles of land, destroying everything in their path. A forest fire was just as deadly. Lightning could start such a conflagration, but he'd spotted the flames minutes before the storm. That fire had been set.

He wondered what happened to Thornton and Jared and hoped they were still alive. But whether they were or not, he was on his own now. He'd wanted a chance at his father's killers and now he had it. Using the arroyo like a conduit, he shadowed Barley and his gang.

He could see a light in the distance. It was a lamp in the window of the Carroway house.

"Looks like somebody's home," said Coble.

"They're sure to have one of 'em watching out for us," said Phipps.

Hendrick was glad that Phipps didn't know just how close that lookout was to him.

"Listen up," said Barley. "We're going to go in easy and quiet. They're not going to know what hit 'em."

"I wish Green was here," said Coble.

"I told you he's got a job to do," said Barley. "Besides, the only one on that ranch worth worrying about is Garcia. Now, quit your blubbering about Green."

When the arroyo started angling to the left, Hendrick could see he was about to lose his cover. They were close to the ranch now, and it was time to fire the warning shots. He decided he wasn't going to waste them by firing into the air. He'd be aiming at the killers.

Their forms were visible in the moonlight, though it was a lot harder to hit a moving target than a stationary one. He reined up and fired at the nearest outlaw. The shot missed but he was already squeezing off another.

Realizing that the shots were coming from behind, the outlaws swung around.

"It came from over there," said Ledoux. "It's got to be Thornton."

"Get him!" shouted Barley.

For the next few minutes Hendrick was busy defending himself. When the pistol was emptied, he used the rifle.

Then, when he needed it the most, he started getting some help. They'd heard the gun battle at the ranch and had come to join in. Not only that, someone was coming from the south. This proved to be too much for Barley and his gang. They took the only way out. With a couple of parting shots, they veered off and headed west for the mountains.

Hendrick was still trying to catch his breath when Thornton rode over to where he was holed up. He saw that Jared was riding double on Coronado.

"You did all right for yourself, Hendrick," said his friend. "You're not hurt, are you?"

"No. But I started it. I was doing some out-riding when I saw the outlaws and followed them. When they got close to the ranch, I fired a warning shot. The thing is, I fired it at one of the outlaws, and he didn't like it."

"You did fine," said Thornton.

Garcia, Wren, and Jim Carroway rode up then.

"I'm glad to see you're all right, my young friend," said Garcia.

"Thanks, but you're no gladder than me."

"Looks like they took off for the mountains," said Wren.

"They'll be back," said Jared. "You can bet on it."

When they were in the mess hall eating a meal that Wren had scrounged, Thornton told what had happened after they'd left him and Jared at the cabin.

"They tried to burn the forest in order to kill us," he finished.

Garcia spat out a word in Spanish that Hendrick was certain was a curse.

"We're going after them, aren't we?" said Wren.

"Look, Thornton, if you're going, so am I," said Hendrick, for he was sick and tired of being left behind.

"The way I see it, we have to. We won't have any peace until they're dead or in jail, and after Barn Oak's escape from Santa Fe, I don't have much confidence in jails."

"We've got to have fresh horses," said Jared.

"See to it," said Thornton. "We pull out of here at dawn."

Shortly before sunup, Cal was at the corral. He'd washed up and changed his soot-stained clothes that smelled of smoke. The horse that he selected was the zebra dun he'd bought from the trader. There was no denying it was a good horse, though not as good as Coronado. The others were there, all except Elizabeth, who'd remained with her uncle.

"Wren," he said, "you're to stay here with Lucinda and the doc. They're going to need you. Hendrick, you, Jared, and Garcia are going with me."

"I've got more ammunition hid out in the barn," said Wren. "Hendrick, help me fetch it. You're apt to need it before this is over."

By the time Cal had switched his saddle to the dun, the others were ready to ride. Lucinda hurried over with canteens of water and bags of corndodgers.

"Thank you," he said.

"It is nothing. Please be safe, all of you."

Being safe wasn't possible. He knew this as he rode out with the three he'd chosen to go with him.

"Those outlaws are apt to be up there waiting for us like we waited for Barn Oak and his pals," said Hendrick, who was clearly worried.

"Maybe," said Cal. "We'll have to keep a sharp look out."

The forest where Barley had headed was untouched by the fire. Thanks to the downpour, the mountain was green for miles before the area of devastation.

"Maybe they're going to make a run for Taos," said Garcia.

The thought had crossed Cal's mind as well, since they were on the trail that led through the mountains to the other side. But he'd dismissed it.

"Barley is wanted by the law and so is Barn Oak," he said. "If he runs, he'll be giving up his chance at the ranch. I've got a hunch that he's not ready to quit yet. Besides, he wants a crack at me."

They followed the outlaws' tracks to the overlook.

"That gang could have watched us leave this morning," said Hendrick. "They could have seen that we're after them."

"They know it anyway," said Jared, looking down on the place that he, too, had tried to steal. "They know how Thornton feels about them. Barley also knows that he's going to have to kill me or be killed."

"It looks like they got off the trail and rode into the wilderness just like we did," said Hendrick.

"I do not like this," said Garcia. "I do not like this at all."

Garcia wasn't the only one. Cal didn't like it either. Still, they had to follow the outlaws' trail wherever it led, or else turn back. He'd made a promise on Tate's grave. He wasn't about to turn back.

Chapter Seventeen

They were riding single file, deep into the wilderness, when Cal heard a shot. The dun screamed, stumbled, and went down. Cal kicked free of the stirrups and threw himself off so as not to get pinned underneath. Shots were continually fired as he rolled into the cover of the underbrush. The attackers were farther south and higher on the slope. They were well hidden. He pulled out the .44 and fired off a couple of rounds in that direction. Garcia was nearby, hunkered down behind a cluster of narrow-trunked aspens. The other two he couldn't see.

"Cover me, Garcia," he said. "I'm going back to get my rifle."

"Be careful, amigo."

While Garcia kept the outlaws busy, he crawled over to the dead horse. As he reached for the rifle, a bullet whipped by his head. He pulled the Winchester from its scabbard and scrambled back to cover.

Hendrick lunged across the narrow path and dove into the brush beside him.

"What are we going to do now, Thornton? They've got us pinned down."

Cal's attention was on the enemy, and he caught a glimpse of dark red among the green. He took aim and fired. The spot of color disappeared. There was no way to know if he'd done any damage.

More shots were fired. Then there was a sudden lull. Cal turned to Hendrick.

"Was Jared over there with you?"

"Yeah, but I guess he didn't want to risk moving from cover."

"Could be he's hit."

"I don't think so. I'd have heard."

Two more shots were fired from the upper slope.

"We can't go forward," said Hendrick. "But we can sure go back. We've got control of the ranch now."

"Barley killed your pa," Cal reminded him. "He killed my friend too, and I'm not backing off."

"Then what should we do?" said Garcia. "We can't stay here much longer. They'll run us out of ammunition and then attack."

Cal was aware of this. He knew he had to act.

"You two keep them busy. Busy enough that they'll think there's three of us."

Hendrick looked over to where he'd last seen Jared. "He's sure quiet over there. He's no help at all."

Cal was thinking the same thing.

"Surely you don't plan to go up there alone," said Garcia. "It is much too risky."

"If you can think of a better way, now's the time to speak up."

"What's the matter down there?" shouted Barley.

"You run into a little trouble, did you?" This was followed by raucous laughter.

Cal had been furious at the slaughter of his horse. He was even more furious now. *Don't let Barley's needling get to you,* he told himself. *You've got to control your temper if you want to get out of this alive.*

"Keep them busy," he ordered.

While Hendrick and Garcia opened up on the outlaws, Cal slipped away. He went back the way they'd come until he was out of sight. Then, with his rifle in one hand and the .44 in the other, he crossed the narrow path and made his way up the mountainside. On foot, the going was rough, for the slope was steep. His plan was to find a position above the outlaws and get the drop on them.

He'd given up on Jared. The man was either dead or else he'd pulled out. Jared had done him a good turn twice. But he wasn't someone who could be relied on. Garcia was a man who was cut from different cloth. When it came down to it, so was Hendrick.

The exchange of gunfire continued as he worked his way southward. At last he was directly above them. The outlaws' attention was focused on Garcia and Hendrick, and they weren't watching their backs. Barley was screened by branches, so Cal couldn't get a clear shot at him. He moved down closer, spotted Phipps, and put a bullet through his shoulder. Phipps swung around but Cal was already on the move.

"He's behind us!" shouted the bearlike outlaw, clutching at his wound. "It's Thornton. I saw him."

Cal fired again. This time Phipps went down.

"Keep the others pinned!" Barley yelled. "I'm going after him."

Fine and dandy. Come on, I'm ready for you.

With Phipps dead, the outlaw ranks had thinned. But Barley was in a temper, and this made him more dangerous than ever.

Cal retreated. He tried to keep cover between him and his pursuer. Barley sounded like a bull moose rampaging through the pines and aspens. He let out a primitive roar of anger when Cal disappeared from his sight. But he stomped on. There was no give in him.

"I'm going to kill you, Thornton!" he bellowed. "Nobody makes a fool out of Matt Barley."

Cal's friends were still exchanging shots with Ledoux and Coble. But none of that was of interest to Barley anymore. He was single-minded. Only one thing mattered—killing the man he hated.

As quickly and silently as he could, Cal moved southward along the edge of the mountain. Barley could be heard lumbering along behind him. Cal risked a quick look back. When he did, he tripped over a deadfall branch. Suddenly he found himself sprawled on the ground. He'd lost his grip on the rifle, and it lay beyond his reach. He could hear the sound of Barley's heavy footfalls as the outlaw came toward him.

"I've got you now, Thornton," Barley said, his voice jubilant as he emerged into plain sight.

Cal grabbed the .44 from his holster and thumbed back the hammer.

"Hold it right there," he ordered.

The big outlaw came to a halt when he found himself looking down the barrel of a Smith & Wesson revolver.

"Drop your gun, Barley! I won't tell you again."

Barley stood there as if frozen in time, glaring at him with hate-filled eyes.

"If you don't drop that gun," said Cal, "I'm going to kill you."

Without warning, Barley roared like an enraged animal and lunged to the side. Cal tried to fire off a shot, but the gun clicked on an empty chamber. He was out of ammunition. Barley was still off balance and struggling to keep his footing when he realized that Cal was helpless. The instant he was upright he turned, ready for the kill.

Cal too was on his feet now. He'd dropped the useless revolver and was running at the outlaw, head low like a butting billy goat. Before Barley could react, Cal connected with his belly and sent him reeling backward. The outlaw brought his knee up and caught Cal on the chin. Then from a sitting position he aimed the big Colt. But Cal was already rolling out of the way as Barley fired. The shot missed by inches.

"I've got you now, Thornton," Barley taunted. "You're making this way too easy for me."

Cal sprang to his feet and grabbed for his knife. But before he could draw it, Barley fired again. The bullet tore through Cal's thigh. He felt the impact but not much pain. Not yet.

"I'll get you good with the next one," Barley promised.

Cal finished drawing the knife and let Barley see it.

"You murdered my best friend," he accused. "I'm not about to let you escape."

Barley aimed the hog leg and Cal threw the knife.

There was the clanking sound of metal on metal and the knife fell harmlessly to the ground.

Barley's laugh lacked any semblance of humor. "Looks like that big medallion I stole from a church is good for something after all. Now it's time to finish you off."

"Drop that gun!" said Jared, stepping from cover just beyond Barley's right shoulder. "I won't mind back-shooting you in the least."

"Why you dirty . . ." Barley started to curse.

"I'll give you a choice," said Jared, cutting him off. "You can surrender and get a date fixed for the hang-man, or you can die right now."

Barley slowly turned to face him, the Walker Colt still in his hand. Cal retrieved his knife as Jared reached out his arm like a duelist and started to pull the trigger. Cal heard the shot, but it didn't come from Barley's gun or from Jared's either. Ledoux had sneaked up behind Jared and had shot him in the back. Jared fired as he was falling, but the shot went wild.

Now the outlaws turned to Cal. It was two against one and he had no gun. He had to act. Without hesitation, he hurled the big knife at Ledoux. It found its mark as he swung around to Barley. He dove for the outlaw's knees and tackled him before he could get off a shot. They were both on the ground, struggling for Barley's weapon. Cal's wounded thigh was on fire now and bleeding profusely. He made a fist and hit Barley hard on the jaw. The outlaw grabbed his neck and began to choke him. His huge hands were like a vice. Cal tried with all of his strength to break his enemy's grip. His throat hurt and he was desperate for air, but Barley was strong as an ox. Shoving his knee into the big man's groin, he forced the outlaw to let go. Cal rolled away, gasping for air. Before Barley could grab him again, he doubled his fist and hit the outlaw hard. Barley went limp.

Cal took his gun and retrieved his own rifle. Then he went to check on Jared. He was wounded badly but still alive, just barely. His lips were moving and Cal bent low in order to hear.

"Elizabeth is safe now, isn't she?"

"Yes. The only one that's left is Coble. Barley's lying over there unconscious."

"He's not dead?"

"No."

Jared reached up with a sudden surge of strength and grabbed Barley's pistol from Cal's hand. He aimed it at the outlaw and fired. Then, having exhausted the last of his resources, he fell back. Cal went over to see what he already knew. Barley was dead.

He went back to Jared and took the pistol from his hand.

"Did I get the job done, Thornton?"

"Yes. He won't cause trouble anymore. Not in this life anyway."

Jared coughed blood.

"I won't ever see Elizabeth again, but tell her it was all for her. You see, I loved her. I truly did."

Those were the last words Jared ever spoke.

Cal reloaded his revolver and made his way down the slope in search of Coble. It turned out that Garcia had beaten him to it. Coble was dead.

"You're hurt," said Hendrick when he saw Cal's bleeding leg.

"I'll fix you up before we start back," said Garcia. "You've lost a lot of blood."

When the bleeding was stopped and Cal wore a fresh bandage, they loaded the bodies onto the horses. Since the zebra dun was dead, Cal rode Jared's mount.

Wren was the first to see them when they rode in. He ran to the triangle that had called the outlaws to dinner and announced their arrival. They all hurried out to hear the news, all except the elder Carroway.

Cal gave Jared's message to Elizabeth. She glanced at what was left of him, a look of sadness on her face.

"He was so misguided," she said. "I wish it could have turned out better for him."

Cal recalled something that Tate had taught him. Actions have consequences. Yet he owed Jared for his life. Not once, but three times. He too wished Jared could have had another chance.

Tired as they were, they organized a burial detail. When the outlaws were buried alongside Jared, who'd redeemed himself, it was Wren who read the words from the Book.

Jim Carroway insisted on looking at Cal's wound when it was over.

"How's your father?" Cal asked.

"Better. With lots of care, he'll be up and around soon."

"That's good news."

"Yes, it is. Listen, my cousin and I haven't had a chance to thank you for all that you've done for us."

"It was nothing," he said. "I was on a mission of my own."

"I know. The five outlaws who murdered your friend are dead now. What are your plans?"

He'd asked himself the same question.

"I don't have any," he confessed.

"Then won't you consider staying on and running the ranch? I have to get back to my practice in Santa Fe, and Elizabeth needs help."

"Elizabeth needs lots of help. The only hand she has left is Wren."

"Do you think you could persuade your friend Garcia to stay? And what about your other friend, Hendrick?"

"I'll ask. I think they might."

"Does that mean you've accepted my offer to become a partner in the ranch?"

A partner? "You mean a foreman, don't you?"

"No. I mean a partner. Do you accept?"

How could he not?

"Yes, I accept. And Carroway, thanks."

It turned out that Garcia and Hendrick did want to stay. Garcia said he needed to keep an eye on Lucinda to see that she didn't get into any more trouble. Hendrick needed a family, and he'd begun to regard Wren, Garcia, Cal, and the others as a kind of family. Cal still felt a sense of responsibility for the boy, so he was glad to be able to watch over him for a while.

"I can't believe it's all over," said Hendrick, as he and Cal were checking on the horses that night.

Cal looked up at the sky, noticing how bright the stars were.

"It's not all over," he said. "The fact is, everything's only just beginning."

Patron: You are invited to make a brief comment or two, signed or unsigned, after reading this book. Your comments may help other readers in their book selection. (Positive as well as negative comments are requested.) Thank you.

_____

_____

_____

_____

_____

_____

_____

_____

_____

_____

_____

_____

_____

_____

_____

_____

_____

_____